SOMETHING
BRIGHT
AND BURNING

ALSO BY WHITNEY AMAZEEN

One Carefree Day

SOMETHING BRIGHT AND BURNING

WHITNEY AMAZEEN

SWAN PAGES PUBLISHING

Published by Swan Pages Publishing.
First Edition September 2022

ISBNs: 978-1-7348997-1-9 (Hardcover); 978-1-7348997-5-7 (Paperback); 978-1-7348997-2-6 (ebook)

Cover Design by Murphy Rae and Ashley Quick
Printed in the United States of America

For Michael

ONE

Two pink lines. That's all it takes for my world to come crashing down before my eyes. I stare in horror at those lines, the indications of a new life inside me and a tiny, beating heart.

Anything, *anything* but this.

The positive pregnancy test taunts me from the cracked white tiles of the bathroom counter. Each pink line is like a middle finger, flipping me off. I pray for one of them to disappear. Just one would make all the difference.

But no. They both remain.

Two pink lines, two middle fingers—one for each candidate responsible for this disaster.

"Everly!" Mariah rattles the locked doorknob to the only bathroom in our apartment. "You done? Amma needs to get in there before we go."

"Just a minute." My voice sounds shaky, so I clear my throat and wrap the test in toilet paper before throwing it away. Wiping the shock from my face, I emerge from the bathroom, wearing my best poker face.

I'm greeted by my younger sister Amma, standing on the other side of the door with her legs crossed. Her wide brown eyes and her lips pinched together in concentration, are almost comical. "That was close," she informs me. "I have to go really bad." She rushes past me, her gaze locked on the bathroom like it's a sanctuary and slams the door behind her.

I squeeze my shaky hands together to hide the fact that I'm trembling and trudge down the hall past our shabby living room, which is a bland square of two worn cloth sofas and stained apartment carpet. Our tiny TV is perched on a modest wooden bookcase, which holds a few of my college textbooks, my worn, thumbed-through Bible, and some romance novels I read for pleasure when I have time. In other words, *never.* Maybe someday I'll be able to spend hours in my room again, flipping through the pages and convincing myself love exists. At least in books.

I step into the narrow, dimly lit kitchen. Mariah grabs her black purse off the countertop and drinks the remnants of her coffee in three gulps. She's dressed all in black today, making her look sleek and sophisticated. Her hair is in a twist, and her dark skin looks so youthful, it's sometimes hard to believe she's my mother. She barely looks old enough to pass for a parent.

She glances at me and smiles, red lipstick stretching to reveal her bright teeth. "You ready, mija?"

"Just waiting on Amma." *Mija,* which means "my daughter" in Spanish, is Mariah's favorite nickname for me. I've always thought it ironic, since our roles often feel reversed, with me being the parent and her the child. Perhaps that's why I think of her as Mariah. Not that I'd dare disrespect her by calling her anything but Mom to her face.

The bathroom door opens, producing my little sister. She's clad in her St. Mary's school uniform, a navy-blue pleated skirt and white polo. "I'm ready! Let's go." She picks up her backpack and panda bear water bottle, carrying it to prevent it from leaking all over her schoolbooks.

"You forgot this," Mariah says. She grabs a beaded pink hair tie from the countertop and crosses the room to fasten it to the end of Amma's braided hair. "There. Now you're the cutest third grader I've ever seen." Her gaze jumps to me. "That is, since you were in third grade, mija." She garnishes the amended statement with a sheepish grin.

I attempt a smile in return, but my heart is still thundering from the pregnancy test I just took. "Whatever. Let's just go." Mornings in our household are always hectic. All three of us have somewhere to be before nine, and there's only one car. Apparently, I'm the only person in this house who can seem to remember that.

I drop Amma off first, since her school is closest to where we live, and because we can't risk tardiness marring her unblemished record. Amma's paternal grandparents only agreed to pay her private school tuition if we promised to get her there on time. "We aren't paying all that money for her to miss out on her education," her grandpa said the first time the school called him with a tardiness inquiry. Since then, we've been careful not to repeat the mistake.

Mariah walks Amma to class as I idle in the parking lot. I watch the exhaust steam float into the crisp summer morning air, dissipating and re-forming like ocean waves on a shore. My mind follows the endless loop. *Steam, evaporate, repeat. Two pink lines. Two pink, motherfucking lines.* I wish I had time to take out my notebook, hidden under the driver seat, and write a poem. But I can't risk Mariah seeing.

Through the window, I see her returning to the car from the stately brick institution behind her with a confident bounce in each step she takes. She smiles warmly at the dad of one of Amma's classmates in passing. He says something to her, and she presses a hand to her chest, utterly enchanted.

When she reaches the car and slides into the passenger seat, I reverse and hit the gas. "Who's getting dropped off next? You or me?"

"Hmm." She flips down the overhead mirror to check her hair and tucks a dark curl back into the twist. "I'm working 'til late tonight, so drop me off and keep the car."

"Did you pack a lunch?" I eye her tiny purse, knowing the answer already.

"Nah. I'll just eat at work."

"You're lucky you work at a diner," I tell her as I speed down the backroads to the hole-in-the-wall where she's been waitressing the past six years, since she and Amma's dad, Chris, divorced. "And not just because of the food. If I were as late to work as you are, I'd get written up."

She shrugs and applies a fresh coat of lipstick. "Not my fault the manager doesn't care."

"Oh, he cares. But his eyes are in love with your body, so he puts up with it."

Her jaw drops and she slaps my shoulder playfully. "Stop it, mija!"

I let out a shaky laugh. By the time I drop her off, she's fifteen minutes late, and I hightail it to the ritzy salon where I work part-time and park. Our car is so old, I have to lock it manually. Not that anyone would give our beat-up sedan another look when it's surrounded by BMWs, Porsches, and Cadillacs.

Purse in hand, I adjust my shoddy heel and speed-walk into The Arbor Salon. The smell of hair products hits my nose as soon as I step into the bright, open rectangle of an entryway. Willow, the manager, is already here, counting the cash in the register. She's got her trusty notebook out, double-checking the calculations she's already made on the computer. I resist the urge to laugh. Willow is over-the-top careful about everything, especially numbers.

"Good morning," I say, squeezing around her to clock in on the iMac at the white, L-shaped front desk.

"How are you?" she asks, tucking her pen into her curly, half-up, half-down hair. She sets down the notebook but stares at it longingly. It's obvious she's itching to continue writing in it with her could-be-straight-from-a-printer handwriting.

"I'm fine." But then I'm not, because Vaughn, the

other receptionist, walks in. My stomach sinks, and the pregnancy test I took this morning flashes through my mind.

Dammit.

"Hey, Everly," Vaughn says, looking straight at me. His dark, closely buzzed hair matches his intense eyes. "I didn't know you were scheduled today."

"It shouldn't come as a surprise. You know I need the hours." I slide past Willow again and cross the entrance to wipe down the glass shelving near the window display. I arrange some magazines in the seating area against the brick accent wall.

Vaughn follows me and does the same. "You work too much," he says, now that we're out of Willow's earshot. "You should make time for other things, too."

"Oh, yeah? Like what?" I don't try to keep the venom from infecting my tone.

"Things like this." He grazes my arm with his fingertips. My skin crawls in response.

"Thanks," I say. "I'll store that info away under *shit I don't ever plan on revisiting.*" I pull away from him. "And by the way, you forgot to clock in."

"Shit. Thanks." As he brushes past me, he grabs my ass. I check over my shoulder to see if Willow happened to catch it, but she's still reading her notes.

I sag in relief and give Vaughn a death glare. Willow has no idea what goes on between me and Vaughn. No one does, and I need to keep it that way. He grins and shrugs helplessly, like he doesn't possess the ability to practice self-control, then clocks in.

I arrange a new batch of hair products on the shelves,

water the plants in tall, porcelain vases, and take a deep breath to rein in my irritation. It's not that Vaughn is unattractive. He has the bad boy vibe down to a *T*. The rebelliousness. The strong jaw. The deep voice. But he's a total pig, so any points he might win with someone else don't even register with me.

When I'm finished with the products, I refill the tea and coffee station in the breakroom and pass the long hall of stylist chairs. It reminds me of a runway, especially with the long, continuous mirrors lining each side of the stretch. There's no shortage of fluorescent lighting to make me feel like all eyes are on me, scrutinizing my every move as I traverse the floor to my place at the reception desk.

Willow stands up to give me her seat. "You and Vaughn can take over up here until your break. I'm going to check inventory."

She walks away as Vaughn advances toward me from across the room. "Ready to make some confirmation calls?" he asks, taking his place at the computer next to me.

I don't answer him but pick up the phone and dial the first number.

A client walks in and Vaughn greets her. "Would you like some coffee, or perhaps a hot mug of tea?" he asks, lifting the corner of his mouth. "We have a new herbal tea. It's lavender with subtle notes of infused bergamot. It's already a client favorite. Would you like to try it?"

Her eyes light up. "That sounds great!"

He nods at her and turns to go make the tea. As he passes me, he says, "Do you think she'll know I made that shit up?" But I don't respond. It baffles me how he can act professional one minute and completely drop the act the next.

"Please call us back if you need to reschedule. Otherwise, we'll see you tomorrow at nine-thirty." I hang up the phone and drop my shoulders in relief. "Last call. Thank God." We've been at this for a few hours now, and I'm more than relieved to be done.

I stand up to go clean the bathroom, but Vaughn restrains me, running his hand up my leg. "Do you have any idea how hot you look today?"

I trap his hand beneath mine and throw it off my leg. "Don't touch me. We're working."

He half-smiles like the words are an invitation. Reaching back down, he touches me again, this time squeezing my knee.

And then I notice Willow standing right behind him. My blood runs cold. How long has she been there? What did she see? She frowns when she notices his hand on my leg. "Everything okay?"

Vaughn removes his hand like I just burned him. "Yeah. She was just asking me if the weird bump on her knee felt normal."

Willow's hazel eyes glow against her brown skin as she searches my face, and I nod. "Probably just a blister or something." My voice is tight and controlled as I try to hide the fact that I'm fuming.

"Ah." Her face clears as she blinks away her suspicion. "Okay. Everly, break time for you."

I don't hesitate. I hop down from my stool next to Vaughn's and clock out.

When I'm sitting at the round table in the break room, I take out my notebook. At first, I'm not sure what to write. There's so much weighing on me, it feels like I can't breathe. But ultimately, I know what the source of my tension is.

I write a poem about Vaughn.

Pretty, Packaged, Poison
by Everly Jean Martin

Vaughn is like the packaged poison
some people consider food.
Visually appealing, a cupcake packed with sugar,
but bad for your health.
Brown eyes, warm as the fire that melts the ice beneath my feet,
a jaw strong enough to weaken knees
but he's still poison.
Because no matter how pretty his wrapping,
he kills me slowly
from the inside
out.

I drop my pen when my phone vibrates on the breakroom table, startling me out of my trance. It's a text from my friend Simone.

Sent you an invite for my brother's welcome-back-from-college party. RSVP so I can start planning.

I put the phone away, making a mental note to respond after work. Since meeting Simone at school last year, she's talked nonstop about how proud she is of her brother, Nick, who recently graduated from an out-of-state university that he got into, courtesy of an athletic scholarship.

I sigh, dreaming about getting a scholarship. After spending hours researching and applying, my frustration from each rejection was like a bitter, tangible substance I couldn't stop tasting. The reason was always the same. I wasn't taking enough classes. But since I still needed to work full-time to help pay the bills, I could only manage one or two classes each semester.

After my break, Willow says, "I think the bathroom might need a quick check. Thanks, Everly."

I nod and hurry past a line of plush chairs to the bathroom. The white tile floor glistens, spotless. I bet I could see my reflection in it if I tried. I sweep anyway and fold the end of the toilet paper into a triangle, exactly how Willow showed me when I was hired.

A knock on the bathroom door makes me jump. It's Vaughn. My stomach turns sour. "What do you want?"

He shuts the heavy, oak door and walks over to me. Each step makes my stomach drop deeper. "Sorry about earlier. I didn't know Willow was there." He snakes an arm around my waist.

"She was literally walking right up to us. How the hell did you not know?" I shove him away.

"Whoa." He holds up his hands. "Why the animosity? I was just trying to mix work with some pleasure."

"Grow the hell up. What are you, twenty?"

"Nineteen." He cocks his head back like he's offended.

"Whatever. You weren't being smart. You could have gotten written up."

He shrugs. "Who cares?"

"*You* should. What if you got fired?"

"It wouldn't really matter. My parents only made me get this job to keep me busy."

"Sounds like you're pretty spoiled." I cross my arms. "If I were you, I'd follow their example and learn to work hard."

He laughs. "Why? I don't need to. They used to say I had to move out by twenty, but they're all talk. They'd never kick me out. You just need to relax, babe."

"No." I cringe at the pet name and shoulder past him. "You may not need this job, Vaughn, but I do." I know how lucky I am to work here. I'm only eighteen and have no salon experience. Still, I'm paid above minimum wage and Willow is flexible with my school schedule. If it weren't for this place, I couldn't help Mariah pay the bills. And without Vaughn, it would be practically perfect.

I'm pretty sure him grabbing me the way he did is illegal, but what I did was worse. If anyone found out, I would most definitely lose everything.

And Vaughn just so happens to be the only witness.

TWO

Dear Everly,

You are writing this journal entry because if what you're about to do ends badly, you'll remember exactly who to blame.

Simone.

Remember that sleepover you two had a couple nights ago? How much fun you had watching horror movies and eating popcorn and ice cream and candy she brought from her house? Well, forget all that. Because the next morning, she told you about that dating app she started using, and how many amazing girls she met. And then next thing you knew, you were swiping through your phone trying to find a good photo of yourself to upload and post to the profile she created with your name on it.

You thought you found the perfect one, but Simone took the phone from your hands, swiping, and said, "That's not a good picture of you. You look angry."

You told her, "Maybe that's just my face."

"It's not," she insisted. Then she stuck her tongue between her lips, pressed tightly in closed concentration, then said, "You always

think the worst of yourself. Here!" She showed you the phone. There was a picture of you smiling. The light was on your face, illuminating your red hair and turning your dark eyes a lighter brown.

You told her, "I do not always think the worst," and captured the phone from her hand and shut it off. "I'm just realistic. There's a difference." You told her you never should have let her talk you into this. That you didn't want a boyfriend.

But she slapped the thin yellow quilt draped across your bed. "Stop it," she said. "You're all work and no play. I'm not asking you to get hitched. Just sleep around a little. Have some fun."

You said, "Having fun isn't going to pay the bills, Simone." Then you brushed your pajamas off as you stood and gathered the dirty dishes from the night before: bowls of leftover popcorn kernels, cups caked with hardened drippings of ice cream. You told her that you don't trust dating apps because pictures lie. People lie.

And of course she didn't listen to you. She said, "Well, none of the girls I've met so far have been liars. Just try it. You might be surprised."

"I'd really rather not," you said. "Take down the profile." You thrusted the phone at her.

But a mysterious twinkle appeared in her eye, and you should have known better right then. "Sorry, can't! I'm late for a date as we speak. If you want to take it down, fine. But at least see if you got any hits first."

You fumbled with the device like it was a foreign object. And you asked her, "How the hell do I do that?"

But she was already gathering her belongings, halfway out the door a second later. "Just fidget around," she told you. "You'll figure it out."

And you shouted, "I've never used a dating app before! At least teach me how to use the fucking thing!"

But she waved. "Toodles!"

You could have strangled her right then and there, but you took a deep breath. Tried to remind yourself why you like her. Simone is nice ... Simone got you the job at the salon when you really needed one ... Simone likes horror movies ... Simone typically comes bearing gifts, like ice cream and candy.

So, instead you offered her a fair threat. You said, "I will disown you as my best friend if you walk out that door."

And she laughed. That's right. Your "best friend" laughed. That bitch. Then she said, "Oh, come on, Everly. We both know that's not true. You're too much of a softie inside. Plus, we'd run into each other at work, and at school next semester, and that would be awkward. You hate awkward."

You tried to call after her, but she slithered out of the room and closed the door. Slithered, like the snake she is.

Scowling, you searched the screen for directions. Some kind of tutorial. You hadn't a clue how to navigate around. It's not your fault that as far as smart phones go, you're embarrassingly out of the loop. Because your family has never been able to afford such luxury. You've always used pay-as-you-go phones to save money, but your job at the salon requires you use a fancy app to keep the stylist's schedules organized, so you were forced to upgrade.

A notification popped up. You had five hits!

"What the fuck are hits?" you wondered, swiping the first one away. But a cluster of hearts exploded on the screen!

It said: You just told Nicolai you like him. Want to send him a message?

And dammit! In that moment, you vowed never to speak to

Simone again. But then a message on your screen stopped you. It was from the guy. Nicolai. It said: Hi.

And the logical side of you was tempted to exit out and forget all about it. You should have been getting ready for work. But curiosity pricked your senses, and against your better judgment, you typed out a response: Hi, I'm Everly.

Unfortunately, you had to pay money to see what he looked like. You didn't have any money. At least, not to spend on an app you barely wanted on your phone in the first place.

A new message then appeared: Want to meet for lunch this Friday? I hate trying to get to know people over text.

And, dearest Everly, you couldn't help but smile. Those words made you feel a little less old-school. But a knot formed in your stomach, because now you had to turn him down. Something you really, really, hate doing.

Not only were you unable to see what he looked like, but you simply don't have time for a boyfriend, or dating. And sleeping around, as Simone suggested, is out of the question. Little does she know, you've had more than your fair share, and not by choice.

Still, you stared at the screen, urging yourself to rip off the Band-Aid and tell this guy you didn't mean to show interest in him. That you actually planned on deleting the app altogether. That you are, as Simone claims, all work and no fun.

You typed back: I'd love to meet on Friday. I'm off at three. There's a neat place across from my work called Beanbags.

Sometimes you really hate yourself.

He wrote: Cool. Love that place! See you there.

And you said aloud, "Yes, you, will, Nicolai. Because I am a *chronic people pleaser who apparently doesn't know the word 'no.'"*

As you write this journal entry to yourself, you're done working, mere minutes away from crossing the street to meet Nicolai. And if you find yourself reading this back, it's probably because things went badly, and you're wondering how things got to that point. Wondering who is to blame. I said it at the beginning, and I'll say it again.

Simone. Simone is the one to blame.

THREE

It's all Simone's fault. At least, that's what I tell myself as I cross the street to Beanbags.

I blink against the bright California sun. The smell of summer is in the air: ice cream, sunscreen, and coffee. I lick my lips, which are dry from nerves, and glance up from the clean, sharply painted lines of the crosswalk against the dark street. A group of cyclists pass Beanbags, hogging the sidewalk and making those who are on foot press their backs against the closest storefront to avoid being taken down. As soon as the last cyclist—a young girl with a stack of books in her bike's basket—passes, I catch sight of my reflection in the window of my favorite café in Los Gatos. I have the same brown eyes and high cheekbones as Mariah, but instead of her dark curls, I have a shock of red hair that often leaves people staring. Red hair I'd like to think I got from my dad.

A pang shoots through my chest every time thoughts of my dad invade my mind. This time is no exception.

But I swallow the feelings and walk up to the sidewalk outside the café. The familiar, brown-shingled exterior of the coffee shop greets me like an old friend. It's lined with green trim and a chalkboard menu is positioned near the entrance.

I hover next to an outdoor table, biting my lip. I should just cancel on this guy. I have no business spending my hard-earned money on overpriced coffee. Also, my free time is limited. If I'm ever going to get through this semester, I need to avoid unnecessary distractions. And romance is nothing but a distraction for me. I'll just be leading him on.

And I'm pregnant.

But I push the thought down. I still haven't processed that little life curveball yet, and now isn't the time.

I take a seat.

The sun beats down on my skin, but in a pleasant way, and there's a light breeze that lifts the leaves of the nearby trees and sends a few straggling red curls into my face. I brush one away from my eyes. My phone beeps a reminder, and I glance at the digital invite Simone sent. It's a classy black and gold invitation that reads *Nick's Welcome Home Party.* I click the "Going" option under RSVP.

I settle into my chair. What if he doesn't show up? And even if he does, how will I recognize him since I couldn't see his photo? I wince, realizing I'll have to leave it up to him to approach me when he arrives. *If* he arrives.

Maybe he's having second thoughts. Or worse, maybe he's already seen me and didn't like the way I looked, so he left before introducing himself. If that's the case, the least he can do is let me know he's not coming so I'm not sitting here, waiting around for him.

I lift my chin and scan the patio area, homing in on a table two away from mine where a man is sitting alone. His head is resting on his folded arms, and I briefly wonder if he's all right. Maybe I should ask him. *No*, I think. *That would be weird. Mind your own business.*

But then he straightens and runs his hands slowly down his face, as if coming up from his resting position is a huge effort. He opens his eyes and locks gazes with me.

I turn away, embarrassed to be caught looking at him, but when a moment passes and I glance back, he's still staring at me. I lift my hand in an impromptu wave, hoping it will make things less awkward. He waves back, and his lips curve with amusement, transforming him from a regular ordinary guy into...I don't know. Something else.

"Bad morning?" I ask. Not saying anything after he just acknowledged me, *smiled* at me, even, would turn things from awkward to painfully uncomfortable.

"The worst," he admits.

Not as bad as mine, I want to challenge. But there's no way I'm telling a complete stranger that I just found out I'm pregnant. So instead, I say, "At least you're alone now."

A funny expression crosses his face. "What makes you think I want to be alone?"

I shrug. "People suck. They're the cause of everything bad."

21

He smiles, but his eyebrows are narrowed. "That's true. People do suck."

"So, what happened?" I get up and cross the patio to sit down at his table. The buzz of socializing with strangers is still fresh in my veins from this morning at the salon, so it doesn't feel like a weird thing to do. Besides, if we're not going to ignore each other, I might as well join him.

But as soon as I sit, I realize I was wrong about his face. Even without a smile, he's not ordinary at all. His thick eyebrows and defined jaw outline his features. He looks like he's in his early twenties and his hair is long and either light brown or dark blond—I can't decide. There's a light spray of freckles across the bridge of his nose. His eyes are a deep blue—but that's not what transfixes me. It's the curious way he's looking at me, like I'm some kind of fascinating creature. I can't help but notice that he's beautiful.

"My parents are getting divorced," he says after a moment's hesitation. The words come out in a harsh sigh, and his head drops when he adds, "And it's my fault."

It takes me a second to remember that I asked him a question. I'm not sure how to respond to that, so I ask, "Why is it your fault?"

He rubs a hand down his face again. "This morning, I accidentally exposed to my dad that my mom is having an affair. I saw text messages on her phone, and … I just lost it. Right in front of them both." The tendon in his jaw flexes.

He looks so distraught that I'm tempted to reach out and pat his hand resting atop the table, but I'm worried it will feel like I'm invading his space. I bite my lip. "That sounds rough. Did you have any idea she was having an affair?"

He presses his lips together and I'm momentarily worried that I've crossed the line. But then he continues. "Actually, I've known for a year, but I never said anything to anyone. When she confessed to me that she was unhappy and thinking of leaving my dad for someone else, I told her she should end it with the other guy. End it with him and stop cheating. But clearly, she didn't. There were ..." He closes his eyes. "There were photos, and graphic messages, and I know I probably should have kept my cool, but I couldn't. I just lost it. And then it all came out, right there at the breakfast table, everything I knew, and now they're splitting up."

"Fuck." It's all I can say, because I'm not sure there's anything else that would make it better.

"What started out as my first morning home in years ended with my dad telling her to pack all her shit and get out." He closes his eyes tightly. "I'm just glad my little sister wasn't home to see any of it."

"I know how you feel," I tell him. "Well, kind of. I didn't cause a fight between my parents. I don't even have a dad. He died before I was born. But I *do* try to protect my younger sister as much as possible. From as many ugly realities of life as I can."

He opens his eyes. They're not just blue, I realize, but ringed with a circle of light green. His gaze is piercing. Unnerving. It's impossible to look away.

"You must protect her from quite a bit."

"I do my best." I shift in my seat to offset the nerves

his stare is filling me with. "But there never seems to be a moment to breathe, you know? It's like there's no end to the awfulness humans cause everywhere they go."

"There isn't an end," he agrees. "But for every awful thing someone does, I like to believe there's something beautiful accomplished by another. You just have to find it."

"Sometimes that seems impossible. Especially when you've only been dealt a bad hand all your life."

The corner of his mouth lifts, making his eyes even warmer. Looking at him feels like being wrapped in a blanket fresh out of the dryer when you're frozen to the bone. "According to the statistics," he says, "you're due for a good hand. There are only so many cards left to play."

"I'd better have two or three decks then. I'd like to think my life is only getting started." I laugh, but I have to admit, his words uplift me somehow. They give me hope, which I have learned can be the most dangerous thing a person can feel. It's so much safer to expect—and count on—the worst outcome.

He grins. "Are you going to tell me your name?"

"It's Everly."

He tilts his head, and his long, dirty blond hair grazes his shoulder. It reminds me of that Norse superhero character from *The Avengers* that Amma likes to practice drawing sometimes. Thor. "I'm not going to lie. I already knew that," he says.

I blink. "How?" I know for a fact I've never seen this guy before. I would have remembered him.

24

He motions between the two of us. "You and I are supposed to be on a date right now."

I glance around us, belatedly remembering the reason I came here in the first place. I turn back to him. He arches a brow in greeting.

"*You're* Nicolai?" My stomach begins tying itself in knots. "I didn't recognize you." It's the closest truth I can offer, all things considering.

"That's funny," he says, "because I recognized you instantly. As soon as I caught you staring at me."

"I was *not* staring."

"You were definitely staring." A cocky grin spreads across his face.

"I couldn't help noticing that you were stressed," I inform him. "Speaking of which, I can't believe you told a blind date about your parents. Aren't you supposed to paint yourself in the best possible light? Make a good first impression?"

"Probably, but there's something about you that made me want to be honest, I guess." He extends his hand to me, and I stare at it, thoughts of my pregnancy swirling in my mind, along with a pinprick of guilt. "We can start over, if you'd like," he says. "Hi, I'm Nicolai."

Hiding a smile, I take his hand, ignoring the tingles that extend up my arm from where our skin touches. "Nice to meet you."

"It's your turn to tell me about your family," he says. "Since I told you about mine."

"No! That's not fair. If we're starting over, that means the conversation we had about your mom's affair never happened. We're meeting for the first time right now."

"In that case," he says, straightening, "I should probably be in a better mood." He dramatically clears his throat, passes a hand over his face, and his expression lightens. "Where were we?"

"Starting over. Nice to meet you, Nicolai. Your name is cool," I say. "What is it? Italian?"

"My family is Russian, actually. And I like your name too. It's pretty."

"Thanks."

"Is your hair naturally that color?" he asks.

Engaging in small talk is hard to take seriously when only moments ago we were talking about his parents' breakup. *Then don't make it fake*, I think. *Pretend this is how the date actually started. What would you tell him?* I touch one of my curls. "Yep, and I'm the only one on my mom's side of the family with red hair."

I see genuine interest in the subtle shift of his eyebrows, like he's being Nicolai again instead of a guy trying to make a good first impression. "What about your dad's side?"

I stare at the table, tracing triangles on the smooth wood surface with the tip of my finger. "I've never met him or any of his family. He died before I was born, and his family doesn't know I exist."

He looks taken aback. "Wow. How can they not know?" Usually people immediately tell me they're sorry for my loss and try to move on quickly, but Nicolai's interest makes me feel slightly more at ease.

"My mother doesn't know them," I admit. "Apparently she met my father at a party and they had a one-night stand. They never talked again, and by the time

26

she found out she was going to have me, he'd died in a car accident. But his name was Leland Jones. That's a start, at least." My heart races as I tell Nicolai this. He's a stranger, and I never talk about this stuff, but he has a warmness that makes me feel comfortable, and dammit, it feels good to confide in someone about my dad for a change—a taboo in my family.

"Have you ever looked him up?" he asks.

"You'd be amazed how many people have that last name." I laugh humorlessly. What I don't tell him is how many hours I've spent looking at the photos of every Jones I can find, trying to find my own features mirrored in the face of at least one. The agonizing thoughts that follow when I inevitably give up, too afraid to message anyone. Because what am I supposed to say? *Hi, I'm Everly. Did you know my daddy?*

Nicolai searches my face, so I straighten my spine. Try to smile. "I feel like we've been talking about me too much," I say. "What do you do for work?"

If he registers the abrupt change in my demeanor, he doesn't show it. "I start a student teaching program at a middle school in September," he tells me. "I want to eventually teach history."

I raise my eyebrows. "I've heard that middle schoolers are, like, the most brutal group to teach. You must really like kids."

"I love them. How about you?"

The question makes my heart race. I blurt out, "I guess I like kids, sure. I actually spent most of high school taking care of my little sister. My mom had to work, and she needed someone to be home with her, so she pulled me out and I homeschooled myself. I started at, like, fourteen, so it was hard, but definitely worth it. I'm just not ready to have one of my own yet. I might not ever be." *Too bad I'm already knocked up.*

He studies me, like he can see through my skin and into my head, where my thoughts lie. It's strangely intimate, and I can't look away.

I can tell he wants to ask me about what I just said but is holding back. Instead, he says, "What's your sister's name?"

"Amethyst, but she goes by Amma."

"Amma? That's cute."

"She's a nut job. Way too mature for her age. It's offensive."

He laughs, letting his head fall back. It's such a real laugh that being the one who sparked it fills me with a sense of triumph. And I feel it then. That he and I could mesh well. Like, our energies match somehow.

"Hey, do you want coffee?" He brushes a strand of hair away from his face. The way his arm flexes in the process catches my eye. "What's your drink?"

"Oh yeah. Thanks, I'll have a vanilla latte." I stand to get in line with him, but he frowns, gesturing for me to remain seated.

"What are you doing? Stay here. I'll get them." He offers me a thoughtful half-grin before going inside Beanbags.

As soon as I'm alone again, I feel the adrenaline rush that comes from talking to someone I share a rare but instant connection with. People like Nicolai are hard to come by. And I want to smack myself. *What the hell am I doing?*

I have no business being here. It doesn't matter how he's making me feel, because no matter how much I want to, I can't erase the second pink line from the test I took this morning. I can't take back the day that caused it. And worst of all, I don't know who the father is.

By continuing this date, I'm totally leaving Nicolai at a disadvantage. I'm leading him on by letting him think I'm ready to start something with him, when in reality my life is a tangled mess that I haven't even begun to sort through.

Before I can overthink it, I pick up my purse and abruptly rise to my feet. I try not to imagine his easy smile slipping away when he comes back to an empty table, holding two coffees.

It's not you, Nicolai. It's me, I want to tell him. But those words have never worked for anyone. So, I don't look back. I grab all my shit, I take a deep breath, and I leave.

FOUR

I both dread and look forward to the two nights a week that I have classes. Dread, because I secretly hate my major. But going to class gives me a chance to leave the apartment. It fills me with a sense of accomplishment, like I'm making progress toward a future, a career that will pay me enough to help Mariah. To get us to a point where we don't have to wonder if there will be dinner, electricity, or gas in the car.

Though it feels like I'm making slow progress, barely chipping away, college is the only hope I have left to hold onto that I won't end up just like my mother someday.

Poor. Pregnant. Alone.

Thanks to my new situation, I'm now tightly packed in all three boxes. I can only hope my hands are strong enough to break myself free.

When I park at my local community college, I stay in the car for a few minutes. I'm so early, the dimly lit parking garage is practically empty.

My date with Nicolai was yesterday, and I haven't been able to stop thinking about him and his contagious smile. The way I felt when we looked at each other. The reason I had to walk away.

I reach under the seat until I touch my notebook. I slide it out from under the seat and open it to the next blank page.

But I can't write.

I don't want to, because writing *the words* would be admitting to myself that they're true, and I'd like to stay in denial just a little longer.

So instead, I flip back to the entry I wrote six weeks ago, on my eighteenth birthday. And I read.

Dear Everly,

So far, this is already the worst eighteenth birthday in history, and it's hardly begun.

Amma is sick. You and Mariah were both scheduled to work, and you couldn't find someone to cover your shift, so Mariah had to stay home with Amma.

Birthday or not, you're terribly worried about the money she's losing out on by staying home. She could probably tell, because she ran her hands over your hair and said, "Today is your birthday, mija. Only good things can happen."

You wish you could be as optimistic as her. But birthday girl or not, you still had to go to work.

And what happened at work this morning is what's making your eighteenth birthday so bad.

You had to open the salon with the new guy, Vaughn, and as you drove to work, you thought of all the reasons you're grateful for your job. You were worried about this month's electric bill, and how we went over budget. Ninety-four dollars over. And the speeding ticket you got last week—the one you got trying to get Amma to school on time—only put you guys in more of a hole.

When you unlocked the back door, all the lights were off inside, so you flipped them on and went to the front desk. It didn't look like Vaughn was there yet, so you set up the computer and counted the money in the register. You looked over the sales numbers from last night and caught an error.

One of the transactions was priced at the stylist discount—fifty percent off. But whoever rang that client up charged them the full amount. You counted the cash, counted it more than once, just to make sure. You couldn't believe your eyes. A hundred extra dollars. The register was over by $132!

And Everly, this is where things got bad.

You thought of something you can never take back.

You thought, "No one would notice if this money disappeared. Not even Willow. Especially if you changed the amount charged to match the discount on the computer."

The thought was like bait, dangling in front of you at such a weak moment. You couldn't stop yourself; you clicked around, changing numbers on the iMac so no one would know, and thought briefly, "Don't do it, Everly, it's not worth it."

But how else were you supposed to come up with the money to pay the light bill?

You pocketed the extra money. You thought, the salon is so overpriced, it probably wouldn't affect anything.

But don't worry, dearest Everly. You're not a complete monster.

A small stab of guilt still sliced through you, especially when you thought of Willow and the owner, Ash. You remembered how they took a chance on you when they didn't need to, hiring you based *on a first impression. Paying you more than minimum wage all this time.*

But guilt was the least of your worries. Because a second later, you heard Vaughn's voice. "What are you doing?"

You hadn't heard him come in, let alone feel him standing close enough to witness what you had just done.

Everly, you were so scared, all the blood surely drained from your face. But you tried your best to sound guiltless, nonchalant, as you asked, "When did you come in?" You didn't know much about Vaughn yet, but you realized that your job was about to become history if he was a decent person.

Carefully, he asked, "You stole money from the register, didn't you?" And then he smiled slowly, and for some reason, it sent chills down your spine.

You were at a complete loss for words, Everly. You thought you were ruined, that if he told Willow, not only would you get fired, but you probably wouldn't be able to get another job again either. You thought about how you could even go to jail. Mariah's face flashed through your mind, her eyes shocked and disappointed. Without your income we'd have to move to a cheaper apartment, and who knows what the neighborhood would be like? Yours is already terrible for the price you pay, but for California, you can't do much better.

You begged Vaughn not to say anything. You even told him you would put the money back. He stared at you for a long moment, then looked you over, top to bottom, and back up again. He said, "I don't know, Everly." The way he said it sounded almost amused, like he wasn't used to having so much power and he liked it. Then he said, "Give me a reason not to tell."

At first, you weren't sure what he meant. You don't have any money, so you couldn't buy his silence. But from the look on his face, you figured it out pretty damn quickly.

You thought of Mariah and Amma. Of how badly they need your income. And you motioned him toward the windowless stockroom.

He followed you inside, and you shut the door and flipped on the light. Being in that tiny room forced you to stand practically nose to nose.

You asked him what he wanted, cutting straight to the chase. "What do I have to do to keep you quiet?" You asked, even though you already knew. To be honest, you were kind of hoping your mind was going to the worst place, praying that instead of what you thought, he was going to ask for something completely different.

He moved a step closer, and his voice dropped an octave. He said, "I'm sure you can think of something." Your heart hammered so hard, you thought you might faint. But he pulled you flush against him and asked, "It's up to you. What's it going to be?"

Oh, Everly. You imagined the worst in that moment: coming home to tell your mother you got fired. Having to cut your meager grocery budget in half to afford light in your home.

In one sense, you were glad the rest happened quickly. But as you're writing this, it's been hours since, and it's still burned into your brain.

Your lips touched. Your shirts came off. He turned you around, and you tried to focus on the wall. Your Abuela always tells you that the mind is a powerful tool, and you tried to use it, staring at the wall, pretending to be someplace else, ignoring his hands on your skin and his jerky, tense movements. But, hard as you tried, your concentration was interrupted by reality.

And the reality is this: Vaughn said it was up to you, but you felt like you didn't have a choice. You did something wrong, and he took advantage of your fear. He wasn't wearing any protection, yet you were the one left vulnerable.

There was a cardboard box stocked with product digging into the side of your bare leg, so you focused on that too, on the pain of the box corner stabbing you.

Despite all your efforts to remove yourself, his hot breath on your neck made the reality of the situation impossible to ignore.

The only consolation is that it ended. After, you covered yourself as best you could, even though he saw everything.

He dressed slowly. He had a stupid, smug smile on his face. And he said, "That was nice. It looks like we both have secrets to keep now."

And ... that's it. He left, shutting the door behind him, and you stood alone in the tiny stockroom, disgusted and appalled at how quickly things had gone from bad to worse.

But what else could you do?

You put your shirt back on and tried your best to smooth down the tangles in your hair. There was a mirror for sale in one of the boxes, and one glance at your flushed cheeks and harried brown eyes proved you weren't hiding a thing. If anything, you only looked even more suspicious.

Your stomach felt heavy, like you'd swallowed a pound of lead. You pulled your pants back on and realized the only thing that felt heavier than your stomach was the back pocket of your jeans, where the stolen one hundred and thirty-two dollars remained.

I shut the journal and try to steady my breathing. It's one thing to rely on the scraps of memory from that day to tell the story. It's another to read my firsthand account, fresh after it happened. I remember writing it, too. Coming home from work and wanting nothing more than to unload my thoughts and intense emotions.

Even though Mariah and I are close, I try not to tell her everything. I often feel like she willingly allows me to shoulder the weight of our family's responsibilities. When she leaves the parent role empty, I have no choice but to fill it. But her blind optimism demands that sort of dynamic between us, since I have no problem seeing the world for what it is.

I know better than to talk to anyone. No one wants to hear about my problems, not really. And I don't want anyone to know them anyway.

When the idea of writing down my feelings first came to me, I went out and bought a notebook that same day.

But for the first few weeks, the notebook remained blank, no matter how badly I wanted to fill it, because it felt awkward to talk to no one. To write to no one. Every time I held the pen, something like stage fright overtook me. I thought, *What do I even write? Who am I talking to? If no one is listening, do my feelings even matter?*

I thought about giving my notebook a name, so I could pretend I was writing letters to someone, but the idea of making up a friend just so I could talk about my thoughts made me feel even more depressed. I didn't have anyone other than myself.

The only person I was willing to depend on was me. Everly.

When I finally accepted that, I was able to write in my notebook. Knowing I would be the only one to see it was freeing. I didn't have to filter anything, because I wasn't talking to anyone but myself, and it felt surprisingly good. So I made each entry out to no one other than myself, and I still do. Anything else just wouldn't feel right.

I still have a few minutes before my engineering class starts, so I flip through the countless entries I've made over time, some written neatly with care and others jotted down in loopy scribbles, as if I was in a race to record the words before they could disappear. I turn to the next blank page and write:

Dear Everly,
 How can having someone inside me make me feel so empty?

FIVE

I have to admit, I was hoping this would all turn out to be a fluke. That the test would be a false positive. Well, *hoping* sounds bad. Expecting is more accurate. I was expecting to *not* be expecting at this point. It's been three weeks since I took that damn test. Three weeks of torture at work with Vaughn, reprieved occasionally by Simone's shifts. But she only works a couple days a week, so torture has become my default state at the salon.

I cringe at the next test I take at home in the bathroom, like I did last week and the week before that.

Positive. It's still fucking positive.

"Dammit," I mutter, tossing it in the trash. I shut my eyes, bracing myself on the cool tile counter with both hands. I take a few deep breaths, and when I open my eyes, they stare back at me in the mirror, red-rimmed, glossy, desperate.

This isn't happening.

I use some toilet paper to dab my eyes and turn the

doorknob quietly so Amma doesn't hear me come out. Mariah is at work, so if Amma needs something, she'll have to ask me. But right now, I need to get these feelings out before I drown in them. I need to write.

The carpet muffles my footsteps as I slink across the hall. Luckily, I have my own room. I would probably have to share with Amma if it weren't for the fact that she's afraid of everything and, even at seven years old, would rather be with our mom than me. And I have to admit I'm grateful. I like my privacy, and I'm going to need it as my stomach gets bigger each week.

I find my notebook stuffed in my underwear drawer. I take it to my bed, setting it on the mattress, and I kneel on the ground to write.

Dear Everly,

You're still pregnant. It's officially time to panic.

Most people in your situation would give abortion some serious thought. And so have you. You've thought about how easy ending this pregnancy would make everything. You could continue going to college without interruption. You'd have the peace of mind that you're doing what your mother didn't, taking steps to break the mold she's made.

You wouldn't even have to tell anyone you messed up, sleeping with two men on the same day. Mariah would never know. Grandpa and Abuela would never find out. Neither would Amma, who looks up to you.

But there is someone who would. Who already does know.

God.

And it's Him you're afraid of disappointing more than anyone else. Not because you're trying to be a "good Christian." That went out the window a long time ago. It's because you love Him. You know he would forgive you, but you love Him so much that the thought of disappointing him hurts you.

And Everly, things might turn out okay. You're still going to college. Baby or no baby, it isn't negotiable. You won't make a child feel the way you always have—like giving birth to you ruined your mother's life. Granted, she was only a freshman in high school when she got pregnant. Not exactly an age for wise decision-making. And it's not her fault Leland Jones died before she could find him and tell him he was going to be a dad. But it doesn't change the struggles she faced by having you. Your grandparents helped, but Mariah is too independent to accept anything she couldn't provide you on her own. Which, unfortunately, isn't much.

Promise yourself, Everly, that you will be different. You will give your child everything you didn't have—healthy, consistent meals. Clothes that fit right, even if they aren't expensive. A safe place to live. You'll give your child your time, because you won't be a slave to your job so you can provide for them. You'll be the responsible one, so they can know what it is to be young.

You'll give them the one thing Mariah couldn't give you, even if she wanted to. A dad. Or at least, you'll damn well try.

Simone's text startles me out of writing. *You're still coming, right?*

Shit. I completely forgot about her brother's welcome home party tonight. I stuff my journal and pen into the waistband of my jeans to take to the car later, and reply, *6:00 p.m., right?*

Her: *Yes. Can't wait for my two favorite people to meet!*

Me: *Are you trying to set us up or something?*

Her: *Of course not. That would be weird. And I'm too selfish to share you. But I still can't wait for tonight!*

I roll my eyes. Neither can I. Meeting her accomplished golden child of a brother is just what I need right now. With my life in shambles, I'm sure the experience will be great.

But then again, who knows? I've been making decent money working at the salon, and I've maintained my grades for my summer classes. Maybe meeting Nick, who has already graduated, will prove to be inspirational in some weird, twisted way.

I go to the kitchen, where Amma is doing her homework at the table. I'll need to figure out somewhere for her to stay if I'm going to make it to Simone's party. "Hey, kiddo." I nudge her. "Have any friends who want to play tonight?"

Amma sighs and looks up from her homework. Her expression is solemn. "You mean anyone with parents willing to babysit me so you can go out?"

I pull out a chair and sit down. "Yeah. Pretty much." I smile brightly at her and prop my head up in my hands, elbows resting on the table.

Amma glowers at my transparency. "I think Jaycee is home, but you really need to stop waiting for the weekend to make me ask my friends to hang out. It makes me look desperate when I don't plan things ahead of time, sis."

"Fine." I tug one of her braids, making her yelp and swat my hand away. "Be ready in a couple hours. I'll call Jaycee's mom."

I park on the street near Simone's house after dropping Amma off. Mariah is working late tonight, so I'll be able to stay a while before picking her up.

The sky is lit with stars tonight, and they illuminate the stone-paved driveway I walk up, along with the well-kept shrubs lining the path to the front door, which is adorned with a homemade wreath. It has a *B* on it for Beckett, Simone's last name.

I ring the doorbell and Simone opens the door. I expect the laughter of guests, clinking of glasses, and music to float around me, but there's only silence.

"What happened to the party?" I step inside. There are black and gold balloons pressed against the ceiling to match the invitation she sent.

Simone chuckles. "Nick is running fake errands for Mom until everyone's here, but he'll be back any minute."

"Oh." I take in her outfit and motion to the beaded silver crop-top she's wearing. It compliments her dark skin well, and her hair is straight, reaching just past her angular chin. "You look hot."

"So do you!" She motions to the simple white dress I took from Mariah's closet.

A cluster of guests arrive then, and Simone breaks away from me to greet them. Mrs. Beckett rounds the entryway corner from the kitchen. "I think it's time to hide, everyone!" She ushers us behind the wall, into the kitchen, where the smell of the food and appetizers arranged on the island is so pungent it makes my stomach growl.

I scan the faces of the guests surrounding me. Most of them are older, probably friends of Mr. and Mrs. Beckett.

I squeeze in between the stainless steel-refrigerator and a forty-something-year-old lady so the view of the front door is almost visible.

"I'm so proud of that boy," the lady whispers. "Pursuing his dream career even though he had the opportunity to run the family company when August and Cheryl retire."

I nod, trying to look enthusiastic, but I have no idea who the hell she is or what she's talking about.

"It's something only an overachiever would do. And those types of people are remarkable."

"Right. Never mind the people who go to college because they have to." I try to mask my irritation, but I'm pretty sure she picks up on it.

"I'm Joanne." She elbows me lightly.

"Everly."

She scrunches her nose. "You're a pretty little thing. Are you a friend of Simone's?"

I nod. "We work together at a salon, but I met her in school last year."

The handle on the front door rattles, and the clanking of keys follows. Mrs. Beckett motions for us to hush our voices, raising and lowering her hands. I peek around the corner. Across the room, Simone appears from behind the staircase and goes to open the door.

Joanne and several other guests shuffle around me, pushing me backwards so I can't see anymore.

"I got the sheets," a man says, "but they didn't have a queen-size bed skirt. Sorry." The sound of plastic wrapping is audible, probably Simone taking the objects from her brother.

"That's okay, Nick. But you forgot something else."

A sigh. "I knew it. What is it?"

Everyone jumps out of their hiding places, collectively shouting, "SURPRISE!"

Everyone floods out of the kitchen into the entryway. I can't see Nick yet because there are so many people crowding around him and Simone, clapping their hands on his back while he laughs. I hang back, narrowing my eyes through the horde, until I catch a glimpse of his face.

When I do, I freeze.

Because as soon as I see him, I recognize his blue-green eyes. His long hair, in a man-bun now, showing off his defined jaw and the arch of his neck.

As soon as recognition seizes me, he looks up, as if sensing my gaze.

Nicolai.

Simone's brother is Nicolai. My accidental date.

A hot wave of embarrassment washes over me. I can't believe this is happening. How the hell did this happen? He probably thinks I'm a stalker or something! And what are the odds that the first guy I go on a date with after swearing off men just so happens to be Simone's brother?

It makes sense that I never made the connection. He must be Mr. and Mrs. Beckett's biological son. He looks just like his mom, and he and Simone—who's adopted— are physical opposites, with her smooth brown skin, chestnut eyes, and raven hair.

Mr. and Mrs. Beckett.

I abruptly recall what Nicolai told me about his mother's affair and cringe. I glance around, realizing for the first time that Mr. Beckett isn't in the room.

Oh, God. Does Simone know? As her friend, do I have an obligation to tell her? "Shit," I mutter.

Simone follows Nicolai's stare and waves me over. I feel like a zombie as I near them, my stomach rolling with each step.

"Nick," says Simone. "This is my friend, Everly. You know, the one I've talked a bunch about?"

"Hi." My voice sounds wobbly.

"Hi, Everly," Nicolai says with just the right amount of friendly interest.

He's pretending this is our first meeting? Huh. I can get behind that. "Hi Nico—" I swallow. "Nick."

Simone brightens. "Good. You guys have met now. I'm going to see if Mom needs help with the food. Be right back."

After she leaves, Nicolai and I look at each other awkwardly. "I—" I begin, then stop. The last time I saw him, he was walking into Beanbags to get me a vanilla latte. "I'm sorry I left that day. It wasn't you."

He furrows his eyebrows. "Then what was it?"

A hand claps him on the shoulder. "My boy, it's so good to see you." An older man embraces him.

Nicolai's gaze flickers away from me as he returns the hug. "You too, Grandpa."

I use the moment of interruption to make my escape. Part of me feels like this is starting to become a habit, at least when talking to Nicolai. I round the corner to the kitchen, where Simone and Mrs. Beckett are handing out custom drinks to guests and preparing hors d'oeuvres on little platters.

"Everly!" Mrs. Beckett hugs me when I appear. My

46

gaze jumps away from her blue-green eyes, identical to Nicolai's but framed by dark hair. I try not to think about her affair, but it's pretty much impossible to think about anything else. "I'm so glad you came. Have some champagne." She hands me a glass, and I gulp from it gratefully.

And then I remember my new body buddy. *Shit.*

I lower the glass to the granite countertop next to me. My body vibrates with tension. Simone frowns at me and sets down a drink tray before she walks over. She touches my arm gently. "You okay?"

"I'm not feeling well." It's not exactly a lie. With everything being thrown at me right now, I can't plaster on a fake smile and socialize another minute. "I think I'm going to take off."

"But you just got here!" She shakes her head. "Just go lie down upstairs for a while. You can use the spare room."

I sigh. "Simone."

"Please, Ever." She makes a pouty face, lacing her hands together like Amma does when she wants something from me. "Pretty, pretty please?"

Thanks to my inability to say no, it works. "Dammit, Simone. Fine." Up in the spare room, I'll be able to avoid explaining myself to Nicolai. For the moment, at least. I follow her upstairs and to the third door down the hall, which is lit with dimmed, ambient lighting.

"Lie down for a minute and come back when you feel better." She shuts the door, leaving me alone in a room with a large bed on a sleek wood frame. There isn't much else in here besides a lamp resting on a low black dresser and a closet with sliding doors.

I fall back against the bed, huffing, and stare down at my flat stomach. It doesn't even hint at what's happening inside me. I know there's still a chance I won't make it to the second trimester. Apparently, miscarriages are way more common than people think. I remember when Mariah was pregnant with Amma, I was so excited to be a big sister that I read three different pregnancy books, which was a lot for me at eleven years old. Those books told me as much.

I stare at the ceiling, listening to the muted sounds of the party traveling up from downstairs. "Hey God," I whisper. "Could you please let me start my period? I'd really appreciate it. I'm not ready to be a parent, and I want to finish college, get a good job, and help my mom with money."

The doorknob turns, and I sit up. It's Nicolai.

His eyes widen when he sees me, and blood rushes to my face.

"Uh, Everly?" He rubs his neck and glances around. "Were you just talking to someone?"

I blink. "Uh, yeah. I was talking to … God." I feel kind of silly telling him but decide it would be much worse for him to think I'm a nutcase who talks to herself.

"… God?"

"Yes," I say simply, like I'm not completely mortified. "It's called praying." *Idiot,* I think. *Why didn't you just say you were on the phone?*

He looks completely taken aback. "I would have

thought praying would sound more, I don't know, formal."

He has a point, but to me, praying is just talking to God. "If you wanted to talk to me, would you read a formal script every single time?"

His lips twitch, like he's holding back a smile. "I guess not."

"Exactly. So there's nothing wrong with the way I pray." Then I realize I'm kind of lecturing him when I'm supposed to be avoiding him. "Is there a reason you barged up here in the first place?"

"This is my room."

My eyebrows fly up. "*Your* room? Simone said this was the spare room. I needed to lie down for a sec."

"That's totally fine. You can rest here, but this is my room. Maybe she called it the spare while I was away at college."

I laugh humorlessly. "That's all right. I'm leaving." I stand up, ready to make for the door, but he shakes his head.

"No, wait." He puts his hand on my arm. "Don't leave because of me."

I glance at his hand, at his arm lined with hard muscle. A wave of desire crashes into me, so unexpected that it's actually alarming. "This is your party." My gaze jumps back to his eyes, and the pit of my stomach aches. "Of course I'm leaving because of you."

His eyes light with amusement. "I thought you said it wasn't me."

"I—" My thoughts scramble together. "It wasn't."

He grins. "I have to know, then. I couldn't stop

thinking about you after I came back to that empty table. Couldn't figure out why you left." His gaze travels down to my lips. "And now you're my sister's friend. Off-limits."

My body reacts to the huskiness in his voice. To the words *off-limits*. What is it about this guy that's turning me on so much? I can't figure it out, but the urge invading my body is making me desperate. And now I'm staring at his lips, which isn't helping at all.

He heaves out a rough sigh. "Maybe you should go."

I nod, ignoring the tightness in my chest at his words. He's right. I need to leave before I do something I'll regret. "Goodbye, Nicolai." I take a step toward the door. *That's right, Everly. Out the door you go.*

And then he touches my arm. "Wait."

When I spin around, his face is closer to mine than I anticipated. I'm momentarily stunned as he leans an inch closer. His hand stays put, rough and warm on my arm.

"I need to get out of here right now," I whisper. But I don't.

I grab his face and kiss him, unable to stop myself. He freezes for the briefest of moments, and then his hands go to my waist, and he's kissing me back.

Excitement, a rush, *something*—builds inside me, so strong my knees threaten to buckle. God, it's so embarrassing. I've never had such little control over myself. I slide my tongue into his mouth and pinch the buttons on his shirt.

And then the fogginess surrounding me clears for a moment.

What am I doing?

Nicolai grunts into my mouth, helping me take off the

shirt, and then his bare chest is revealed, hard and tan and smooth.

I yank his hair out of the man-bun. It falls around his face and to his shoulders. I walk him backward until we fall on his bed.

The kiss breaks, and he pants. "Ev, what are we doing?"

I shut him up by kissing him again. I can't explain what this is because I don't know myself. All I know is I've never needed hands on my body like I do right now. I've never experienced the closeness of someone feeling like a drug.

"I have no idea," I whisper. "None." I grab his hand, guiding it along the smooth skin of my leg.

His eyes darken with desire, but he shakes his head a little, as if to clear it. "We should stop."

"I know we should stop." My voice is strained when I add, "But that doesn't mean I want to." I don't wait for him to think it through, just kiss him again, moving his hand up until it reaches the soft material of my underwear. His fingers remain on them and his other hand reaches up to cup my swollen, tender breast. I gasp in surprise. In satisfaction. The straps of my white dress slide down my shoulders. His thumb lightly glides across my bra before he pulls it away. Our eyes met. His gaze is questioning, almost like he's asking permission to continue. So I lean into him, pressing my neck against his lips. *Permission granted, Nicolai.*

Someone knocks on the door. "Everly?" Simone calls softly.

"Shit!" he exclaims.

I push him off, grab his shirt, and crawl under his bed. I don't know why I took his shirt. It was an instinct. And now he's sitting on top of his bed, alone and shirtless. I smother my laugh with the damn shirt.

The door opens. "Nick?" Simone asks. "What are you doing here?"

He clears his throat. "I had to change my clothes."

Simone pauses. "Have you seen Everly? I left her up here a while ago."

"Everly?" he repeats, sounding pretty convincing. "Nope. I haven't seen her since you introduced us."

"Okay. Thanks." The door closes, and I'm about to crawl out from under the bed when she opens it again. I slam back down on the ground. "By the way," says Simone, eyeing him suspiciously, "you should probably lock the door the next time you're ... changing."

She shuts the door again, and I wait for a minute before scooting out from under the bed this time. I stand and shoot Nicolai a sheepish smile as I hand him back his shirt.

"Thanks," he says sarcastically. But he's not mad. He's smiling, like this whole thing is amusing.

"I'm sorry," I say breathlessly. "I don't know what came over me."

He arches an eyebrow. "You're going to have to fill me in," he says. "As far as I know, you left in the middle of our date without an explanation. *But it wasn't me.*" He emphasizes the last sentence.

My cheeks burn, because it really is a lousy excuse.

"And then as soon as I find out you're friends with my sister, you practically jump me."

I glance at my hands. Tears build behind my eyes because he's right. I do owe him an explanation. *Do not cry, Everly.*

"Is there something," he continues softly, "I'm missing?"

I might as well tell him the truth at this point. Part of me even wants to sabotage this thing between us, to give him a reason not to want me anymore. He'll never look at me the same way again after tonight, anyway. I'm his sister's friend. Off-limits. Going on the offense to keep myself protected is appealing, and I don't have time for someone like him in my life right now. Why give him false hope?

"I'm pregnant." It's the first time I've said it out loud and doing so somehow makes it more real.

Maybe that's why I couldn't keep my hands off him. Hormones or some shit. Mariah's baby book mentioned something about pregnancy changing a woman's sex drive, although it said most women experience a decrease in libido. It figures that I would be one who gets the opposite.

He tilts his head. "Come again?"

"I found out the morning of our date. That's why I left. It was too late to cancel, and when I met you, I liked you, so I left."

"Because you're pregnant." He says the words like they taste foreign.

My face burns. "Yes." I retrieve my purse from the floor. "That, and I really don't have time to date." I glance at the time on my phone. My mom will be off in twenty minutes. "Speaking of time, I have to go."

"Everly, wait." He reaches out, but I don't wait. It's time to pick up Amma. It's time to pick up my mom.

And it's time to stop pretending.

I park outside Jaycee's house and sit, regaining my composure.

What the hell *was* that with Nicolai? I barely know the guy. I shouldn't be this worked up over someone I've spent so little time with.

I look at myself in the rearview mirror. My cheeks are flushed, my hair is messy, and I look guilty as hell. It's like I'm in high school all over again.

"He's just a guy," I tell my reflection. "Someone you can't have. That's why you can't stop thinking about him."

But the words don't help. I reach under the seat where I left my journal. I write:

a touch
so fleeting
a soft, simple feeling
that leaves me
r e e l i n g.
Oh how
oh
how
will I recover?

SIX

"Amma, come help me pick up these markers!" Mariah is on her hands and knees when I come home from my night class on Wednesday. She fishes a marker cap out from under the couch.

"Need help, Mom?" I drop my backpack on the ground.

She stands. "No, mija. Go get your sister. She made the mess, so she can clean it up." She rubs her lower back. "I'm going to lie down."

"You okay?"

"Dolores from the diner quit a few days ago," she says. "I've had to cover her tables. My back is sore. That's all, mija."

I pick up my bag. "Go sit down. I'll make Amma clean up." I check Amma and Mariah's room and my sister is on the bed, drawing a picture.

I lean against the doorframe. "Mom's out there busting her back, cleaning up your marker mess."

"Oops. Sorry." She finishes up the line she's drawing, tongue sticking out between her lips in concentration. Then she sets everything down and rises. "I got it."

"Mhmm." I watch her skip to the living room where Mariah is now sitting on the couch. Instead of following her, I walk to my bedroom, position my backpack in front of the door, and take out my notebook.

Since reading about the first part of my birthday last month, I've felt an itch to finish reading the rest. It's all committed to memory, of course, but reliving it that day brought back emotions I wasn't prepared for. Since I'm still pregnant, I think reading the second part of my birthday might help me sort out my emotions. Or at least, help my denial shift into something like acceptance.

I lie on my bed, using a pillow under my knees to get comfortable. I find where I left off when I started reading a month ago.

Dear Everly,

Your eighteenth birthday is officially over, and guess what? Things only got crazier after Vaughn caught you stealing money this morning. You almost didn't go out with Simone because you were so upset about what happened at work, but then you remembered Mariah's words, that only good things can happen on your birthday. And even though she'd already been proven wrong from the moment you went into work, dammit, you still wanted to try.

You met up with Simone at an elegant bar on the same Los Gatos block as The Arbor Salon. As you stood hand in hand outside, waiting to go in, you told her it was finally starting to feel like your birthday.

She smiled like you were being silly. "Why?"

But you just shrugged, trying not to stare in the direction of the salon. The memories from earlier, with Vaughn, in the stockroom made you feel queasy. You could still feel his hands on your skin, despite the shower you took before meeting Simone.

"You have your fake ID?" you asked. Not that she needed it. You both took two shots before arriving, thanks to the bottle of vodka Simone has been hoarding in her room all week.

But she pulled her fake out of her phone wallet and flashed it at you. The picture was clearly her: white teeth, glowing brown skin, and rich, glossy bobbed hair. At least she had an actual fake ID. You had to use your mom's old driver's license. You still feel guilty about her having to pay for a replacement when it went "missing." But you considered your action justified, given that your life is all responsibility and very little fun.

You were worried you wouldn't be able to pass her photo off as yourself, since her hair is dark brown and yours is red. But it was fine, probably because she had you when she was younger than you are, and you're just similar enough in appearance for it to work.

You and Simone got past the bouncer easily. Both of you looked stunning, done up to appear older and dressed in your nicest clothes. You wore a red dress that matched your hair and lips, and Simone had on a white one that made her skin look irresistibly soft.

When a song you both liked came on, you headed straight for the dance floor without a word passing between you. As you drunkenly swayed to the music, you couldn't help but notice several men watching, and Everly, it pleased you. Since breaking up with your high school boyfriend, you've been lonely. Too busy to date, the awful idea that you've become undesirable has been invading your thoughts. Until this morning, with Vaughn.

"*Come on,*" *said Simone. "Let's see if we can get someone to buy us a drink.*"

You followed her to the bar, where she sought out the most desperate-looking dude in the room and talked to him like they'd been friends for years. You lingered behind her, tuning out their conversation. A moment later, she produced two margaritas, paid for by the man, and handed one to you. "Drink up, bitch."

And you did.

An hour and several drinks later, Simone was too sloshed to function. You helped her into the Uber you called and debated whether or not to join her. You ultimately decided to live a little since it was your birthday. But you made Simone promise to text you as soon as she got home.

She nodded halfheartedly and shut her eyes. "Happy birthday, Ever. Love you."

"Love you more," *you said. After her driver left, you went back inside and wondered what the hell you were supposed to do now that she was gone.*

A man was sitting alone at the bar, and you took the seat to his left. Why the hell not? He looked nice enough. He had short brown hair and was wearing a nice button-up shirt.

"Hi," *you said, nudging his shoulder. "I'm Everly.*"

He turned to look at you, and the corner of his mouth turned up a little. "John."

"I like your shirt."

He chuckled. "You look too young to be here."

"I'm not too young. I turned twenty-one today. It's my birthday." It was a half-lie of course, but he didn't have to know that. He seemed a little like a goody two-shoes, and the last thing you wanted was for him to alert the bouncer that you were underage.

He shook his head, grinning a little. "Happy birthday. Everly."

Something about him felt sad. You still can't put your finger on it, but there was something inherently melancholy about the set of his eyes, the way even his smile didn't look happy.

"How old are you?" you asked. Not a single wrinkle lined his face, and you guessed he was probably in his late twenties.

"I'm thirty-three," he said. "Which is too old for you."

You laughed. "Who said anything about you being for me?" You raised an eyebrow mischievously. That margarita was definitely still going strong. "You came up with that all on your own."

John laughed and shook his head a little. "As fun as this is, I have a feeling you're a world of trouble, little girl."

"I'm going to take that as a compliment." You placed a hand on your chest. "You clearly have no idea how much fun trouble can be."

John stared. "Dear Lord."

You giggled, and took a swig from John's drink, hardly tasting anything, though it appeared to be Jack and Coke. John didn't stop you, so you finished it, enjoying the way he watched you do it.

"So, John." Your voice sounded slurred. "What brings you to the bar tonight? Scoping out the ladies? Are you single?"

His smile faded, and he pursed his lips. He stared at his hands for a moment and then looked back at you. "Today would have been my third wedding anniversary, but my wife passed away last year. Cancer."

And Everly … your heart broke for him then. You didn't know what to say, but you tried. "I can't even imagine how that must feel. I'm sorry."

He waved away your sympathy and took a deep breath. "I hope you never find out how it feels."

"If it makes you feel any better, which I'm sure it won't, this has been my worst birthday ever."

"Why?"

You leaned in close to whisper in his ear. "I stole money from work, and my coworker caught me."

His mouth fell open in surprise. "Are you serious?"

You nodded, pressing your lips together to keep from laughing.

He chuckled. "I can't believe you just told me that."

You shrugged, discretion beyond you at this point. "Where do you live?"

John appeared to be pondering his answer. If there was a time for him to put a stop to whatever was happening, it was then, and he knew it. You could see the struggle behind his eyes.

He finally said, "Want to come and see?"

Did you ever? "Yes!" You grinned and hopped down from the barstool.

He paid his bill, linked his arm through yours, and led you to the parking lot. Your eyes widened when he unlocked a shiny black two-seater Porsche 911. A fucking Porsche!

You pointed at it. "This is yours?"

"It is."

"I've never seen such a nice car up close, and I'm a car person."

"Well, hop on in." He opened the door for you. "You'll want to see it really up close."

You didn't think twice, Everly. You got in, sniffing the leather as subtly as you could so you didn't seem like a weirdo. "I could get used to this," you told him when he was buckled up next to you.

He drove through downtown Los Gatos, white-light-strung trees framing the street. Pedestrians weaved in and out between cars, not a care in the world and dressed like they belonged, like they grew straight from the ground of that expensive city.

He headed for the hills, and your anticipation expanded. The number of houses became sparser, and you briefly wondered if John was a serial killer disguised as a nice guy or something. But he eventually pulled into a driveway, and your jaw dropped.

You said, "You must be stopping for directions, John, because this isn't your house."

"It isn't?" He flashed the headlights, illuminating the mansion and squinted through the windshield. "I'm pretty positive this is where I live, Everly."

You still have no words. What is it like to have this kind of money? You sure would like to find out some day.

He turned to you. "Would you like to come inside?"

"Are you kidding?"

For the first time, there was hardly any sadness in his eyes.

You walked up the driveway, which covered an area larger than your apartment. His house was perched on the hillside, overlooking Silicon Valley. He entered a code into a digital pad beside the door, and a green light flashed. When he opened the door, you stepped inside and gasped. It was nicer than an ad for home décor, even though the space had a minimalist feel to it. There wasn't much furniture. Modern statement pieces hung on the white walls, which blended seamlessly with the bright floors. Dark marbled counters and glass-doored cabinets gave the eye places to rest. There was no separation between the living room and kitchen. It was one giant space that made the area feel open and inviting. "What do you do for work?" you asked.

"I'm a pediatrician."

"Doctor John ..." You waited for him to fill in the blank.

"Taylor."

"John Taylor." You tested the way it sounded aloud.

He laughed. "Do you want anything to eat or drink?"

"Water is fine."

He shuffled to the kitchen and filled a glass with water and handed it to you without waiting for a response. Looking back, it was probably made of fucking crystal.

"Thanks." You glanced around. "Can I see the rest of your palace? Where's your room?"

His eyebrows flew to his hairline. "Uh …"

You rolled your eyes. "Oh, come on. I'm not that young. Don't pretend you invited me over for charades."

"You look young for twenty-one," he said pointedly. "Should I be worried about your daddy coming to beat my ass later?" He was serious under his attempt at humor.

"No, because I don't have one."

What else were you supposed to say? That he died before you were born and Mariah doesn't even have a single photo? That there was a brief period when you considered Amma's dad, Chris, as yours since he came into your life when you were pretty young, but any connection you had with him was severed when he walked out on you, Amma, and Mariah?

It was nice having a father for a while, but the feeling of not having one is more familiar. It's your normal.

The humor in John's eyes dimmed. He gazed at you for a long moment and then planted a soft kiss on your lips. "Come on," he said, taking your hand and leading you upstairs.

You were excited, wondering what on earth his bedroom would look like with a living room and kitchen that nice, but surprisingly, it was relatively simple. The walls were off-white, and the hardwood floor matched the one downstairs. The giant bedframe was made of blond wood, and his comforter was an inoffensive gray.

You weren't as drunk as before, but still tipsy when John gestured you inside, and you sprung onto the bed, bouncing as the mattress moved under you. He tried not to smile and failed. You must have seemed like such a child to him, but you couldn't help it. You'd *never seen such luxury in person before, besides the salon you work at. But this was different. John actually lives in that house!*

You patted the bed, inviting him to join you.

He lay down carefully, like he didn't want to disturb the stillness of the bed.

But you'd had enough of his caution. You slid on top of him, kissing him slowly at first and then more desperately. He wove his fingers lightly through your hair, grunting when you bit his bottom lip.

He pulled away. "Are you sure about this?"

You thought of Vaughn, Everly, and how you wanted to erase the feel of his rough hands on you. John appeared to be everything Vaughn was not: gentle and soft, unsure and reluctant, whereas Vaughn was adamant and aggressive.

You needed this.

And looking at the sadness lingering in John's eyes, like it had attached itself to him and found a new home, you could tell there was an eagerness in him to forget a thing or two as well.

So you gripped his shirt firmly and said, "I'm completely sure, John." Breathing heavy, you kissed him again. "Please."

As he stood you up and undressed you, the thoughts of Vaughn began to slip away. His soft touch replaced Vaughn's unyielding persistence. Even though you made a deal with the devil, this man felt like a little piece of salvation. And as he obliged you with each hesitant thrust, you clung to him like the lifeline he was, refusing to let him go.

I set down the journal. "I'm such an idiot." Stuffing it under my bed, I try to hold back my tears. I never should have slept with both of them on the same night. Now I have no idea which one of them is half responsible for this mess.

And it didn't end on my birthday, either. It's been six weeks of the same bullshit. Me sleeping with Vaughn in exchange for his silence, and occasionally using John to mask the pain, to fool me into believing I still have control over my life.

I'm not sure reading about the rest of my birthday helped. I'd been hoping for some clarity on how things turned out this way. But now that both sides of the story are fresh in my mind, I'm even more lost than before.

I need to talk to the dads.

If this pregnancy insists on continuing, I need to consider all my options and fast. And the first step is figuring out which man is the father of this baby.

SEVEN

I'm distracted all morning at work the next day. Last night, I texted Vaughn and John, asking them to meet me at Beanbags across the street when I'm off. The same place where I had my date with Nicolai.

I try to push him out of my head while I ring up a client, but it's impossible. I never confide in people. I never vent. I only complain about life in my journal. But the very first time I saw Nicolai, I *talked* to him, spoke to him about things I normally only write down.

The more I try not to think about him, the more I want to talk to him again.

"Hey girl," Simone says, scooting me away from the iMac so she can clock in.

"Hi," I say, standing straighter. I haven't seen her since Nicolai's party last week, and I'm worried she's been mad at me for leaving without telling her. Though not as mad as she would be if she'd seen the way I coerced her brother onto his bed and kissed him with a passion that shouldn't have left me feeling ... I don't know. Something I've never felt with anyone else. How could a few stolen, clandestine moments leave me feeling so much more intense than anything else? The invasiveness I experienced with Vaughn, and the comfort I felt with John, are nothing, *nothing* compared to this. To what I'm feeling now.

"Where have you been?" she asks, sounding concerned.

I finish ringing up the client, say goodbye to her, and turn to Simone. Guilt stabs me. I'm such a shitty friend. Running out on Simone's party after she did everything she could to make me feel comfortable enough to stay was inexcusable. As much as I want to explain myself, there's no way I can tell her about my date with her brother. Not after he and I pretended not to know each other right in front of her.

I latch onto the other huge secret I've been hiding, knowing it's a good enough excuse for the shoddy way I've been acting. "I'm pregnant," I blurt.

Her eyes round into saucers. *"What?"*

I nod and glance over my shoulder, even though I know Vaughn isn't scheduled today. Still, I'm not ready for him to find out until I'm sitting at a table with both him and John together. I don't feel comfortable telling Vaughn while we're alone. I have no idea how he'll react. At least that way, John will be there to buffer any sort of explosion.

Simone grabs my arm. "Who's the father?"

I sigh. "I've been asking myself that question since I found out."

She covers her mouth with one hand and then drops it. "Have you told your mom?"

"Of course not." I give her a withering look. "Not until I know whose baby it is. But honestly, telling her sounds more impossible than getting rid of it."

"But you aren't having an abortion, are you? I mean, you are religious."

I can't help but find her response kind of funny. As if religious people don't make mistakes? Like we're supposed to be perfect or something? I know lots of religious folk who walk around acting and pretending they're perfect and never make any mistakes or—God forbid, *sin*—but I would have thought non-religious people could see through that and realize we're just people trying our best to follow the God we love. Especially Simone.

"I'm full of mistakes, Simone," I say. "I had sex before marriage, too. That's technically a sin. Anyway, no I'm not having an abortion. There's only one way I'd even consider it."

She crosses her arms. "Which is?"

I stare at the ground, my vision blurring. "If the father doesn't want the child."

———

Leave Me Lost
by Everly Jean Martin

I wish I could remove my heart from my chest,

& bury it deep inside the ground
where no one else can find it.

Because if they did
if they found my heart
stole my heart
broke my heart,
I would have to climb inside the grave
& hope oblivion finds me first.

I glance up from my notebook in time to see Vaughn approaching my sidewalk table outside Beanbags after work. He holds his head up, gaze locked on me as he walks over, then leans down to plant a wet kiss on my lips and sits down. *What the fuck?*

"Hey, babe. What's this about? Couldn't wait 'til later for more of me?"

I stare at him in disbelief. He can't possibly think I've been *enjoying* our arrangement. It's been almost two months since we started sleeping together, and every time has made me want to rip my skin off afterward. "I need to tell you something, but I'm waiting for someone else to get here first."

Vaughn frowns. "Someone else? Simone?"

I open my mouth to explain and see John, crossing the street toward us. When he notices I'm not alone, his expression grows uneasy.

"Hi, John," I say, "thanks for coming." It's more of a relief to have him here than I anticipated, and that's obvious by the sound of my voice. Now I won't have to be alone with the leech. "John, this is Vaughn."

John glances at him briefly and sits. "Everly, what's this about?"

Dread races through me as I take in the two of them. It's almost powerful enough to send me running.

I swallow my fear and say, "There's something you both need to know." I take a deep breath. "I had unprotected sex with both of you on the same day."

Vaughn's face reddens. "What did you say?"

I'm pretty sure he heard me perfectly. I can't even look at John, afraid of what I'll see on his face. A long stretch of silence follows. I want to fall off a cliff.

This sucks.

Vaughn finally breaks the silence. "I swear, if you're about to tell me you gave me some kinda STD, I'm going to—"

"You're going to what?" John asks him, raising his voice slightly. "What will you do?"

I hold up both my hands. "Please. There are no STDs as far as I know. I should probably get tested, but that's not the reason you're here. I'm pregnant."

They stare at me, silent, expressionless. Until they aren't.

Vaughn shakes his head in obvious denial, and John's mouth wobbles into a disbelieving smile.

"You're getting rid of it," Vaughn says immediately, "or I'll tell Willow you stole the money."

Something like hysteria catches in my throat. I should probably be relieved he wants me to get rid of it. It's the rational thing to do, of course. But the thought of him forcing me to make such an important decision—of him

69

declaring the verdict *for* me—all for the sake of keeping my job …

I hope like hell the baby isn't his. I wonder if he'll even give me a chance to find out before opening his mouth.

I can't let his threat be the motivation for such a permanent, life-altering choice. Tears cloud my vision, so thick I barely register the murderous expression on John's face.

"If you dare talk to her like that again, I will have you arrested. Blackmail is a crime," John growls through clenched teeth. "She is not having an abortion unless she wants to. Do you understand me?"

"Go ahead and try," says Vaughn. "I'll just report you as a sex offender."

"I'm eighteen!" I yell, panic seizing me. "I have been since I met you both, Vaughn, legally an adult!"

"Eighteen?" John cries. "You said you were twenty-one!" He rubs his face and then takes a deep breath, as if to center himself. "Wait. That's not what's important here."

Vaughn's face is a mask of hard lines. "I'm not afraid of you," he tells John. "Let's go. We'll do this right now."

John shakes his head. "Watch yourself. I have a feeling prison would suit you, and I have a cop friend who owes me a favor."

Vaughn reins in some of his anger and faces me, hatred in his eyes. "What the hell, Everly?"

I gape at him. "This isn't all my fault. You chose not to use a condom."

"We were in the moment," he insists.

John crosses his arms, looking resigned. "I have no excuse. I should have thought to ask you about birth control." He glances at me. "But would you believe me if I told you I hope it's mine?"

My heart flutters for a moment, not with feelings for John but with hope that maybe there's a chance this could work, that things won't turn out to be a complete disaster. Maybe the baby will be his. He has money. He's kind, and successful.

And way older than you, Everly.

But I put the thought out of my head. If he is the baby's dad, Mariah will get over that little fact when she finds out how ideal a candidate he is to be a father. My life could possibly continue as planned. John could afford to hire a nanny while I finish school. I could still have a career, and all my hard work wouldn't be for nothing.

"You can have it, even if it's mine," says Vaughn. "Screw this."

My heart sinks. If it's Vaughn's child, I don't know what I'll do. "I'm going to get a DNA test done," I tell them. "But I'll have an ultrasound done first to make sure everything's healthy in there, and then we'll talk about our options after that."

Vaughn abruptly stands, his chair scraping back loudly. He glares at me for a long moment and then walks away.

The tears that have been building behind my eyes finally spill over. This is all my fault. If I hadn't stolen that money, none of this would have happened. I wouldn't have felt the need to keep Vaughn quiet by bribing him with sex. I wouldn't have felt disgusted after that and sought out John, hoping to somehow erase the sting left by Vaughn's touch. And I definitely would not have gotten pregnant.

A sob escapes me, and John moves to the chair next to me, rubbing my back lightly. "It's okay. We'll figure this out."

"How? How will this be okay?"

He sighs deeply. "I've always wanted kids, but my wife couldn't get pregnant. And then she got cancer. Things never turn out the way we expect."

"No," I say, meeting his eyes. "Things never turn out the way we *hope*."

I go home after John finishes comforting me. While I'm still not totally at ease, it felt good to have his support. Better than good actually—his response was everything I could have hoped for and more. If he's the father, there really won't be much to worry about.

I have school tonight, but I need to pick up Amma and Mariah first. I have a few hours until then, and I need to write in my notebook. Today has been a complete mess, and my heart feels like it weighs more than my body can support.

I take the journal to my room and shut the door even though no one's home. I press my mouth to a pillow and let out a scream. It feels good.

Before I write anything, I flip to where I left off reading. I don't know why I'm torturing myself with reliving what happened after my birthday six weeks ago, but I can't stop. Maybe I'm a masochist.

Dear Everly,

The drive to church was silent this morning. Mariah definitely knows something is up.

After you didn't come home two nights ago and then showed up at the ass-crack of dawn yesterday morning, she has every right to be suspicious. In the car, her silence was deafening, but she still hasn't asked or outright accused you of anything. Maybe she doesn't want to know what happened.

And thank God, because there's no good way to tell her you had sex with two different men on the same day. So you'd be forced to lie to her if she asked.

In the car, Amma started complaining about a stain on her church dress, pointing to it in disdain. Has she no idea how strapped you guys are right now? Doesn't she realize Mariah's heart is too big to ignore her material desires, so it will only make her feel bad?

And sure enough, after she complained, Mariah said, "Sorry, sweetie. We'll have to get you a new one soon."

And Everly, you got so annoyed because she knows damn well there's no money to buy her a new dress right now. There's barely enough to put gas in the car and food on the table.

"God doesn't care what you're wearing, Amethyst," you muttered, causing her to downcast her face and pout. You felt kind of bad because you knew it was harsh, but you were still feeling disgusted with yourself for your behavior on your birthday. Sleeping with Vaughn in the morning and John that night made you feel dirty in a way you never have before.

Not just guilty, but actually dirty.

You really wish you had used a condom with at least one of them … especially Vaughn. But in your defense, you haven't had a boyfriend in a while, so there was no reason to stay on birth control. After all, it's not like you knew you'd be getting blackmailed for sex when you woke up that morning.

You got to church just in time to sing, your favorite part. Closing your eyes and feeling the music puts you in a sort of peaceful trance. It's the easiest way for you to feel close to God. And after what happened on your birthday, you're craving that more than ever.

But then your phone vibrated in your pocket. You pulled it out inconspicuously and read the text from Vaughn. It said, "I want to talk to you."

You hadn't spoken to him in two days, not since the morning of your birthday, when you were in the stockroom. You avoided him the rest of the day and didn't hear from him yesterday. He got what he wanted, so you couldn't fathom what more he wanted to talk about now.

And then another text came through, this time from John. It said, "Hey. Can we talk?" Like, seriously? What the fuck?

Mariah saw and cleared her throat, glaring pointedly at your phone. You put it away, getting back to the music, but the rest of the service passed in a blur with those text messages weighing heavy on your mind.

Out in the parking lot, you checked your phone again. There was another text from Vaughn that said, "Come to my house or I'm telling Willow." And Everly, you thought there had been an agreement. The sex that morning was a bribe to keep his mouth shut. He wasn't supposed to continue making demands.

But your stomach feels heavy as a wet blanket, now that the dawning realization has finally washed over you that yes, yes he does get to make demands. Because you have nothing to hold over his head. You took the money. Which means he basically owns you if you want to stay employed. And you don't just want to, Everly. You need to.

So you told Mariah that you needed to meet a friend and asked her to drop you off. She agreed to, but just barely. You could tell she was still suspicious. And she has every right to be, but it seemed like she was trying to do something nice for you anyway by letting you go.

Keeping your job is technically nice. You just wish there was a different form of job security you could rely on.

You just thought of a poem that sums up how you felt in that moment, thinking of Vaughn and knowing what he was going to want from you. It goes:

My sadness hangs above me
like a curtain
an oil painting
a cloud
and you are the storm
holding the hammer
& the nails
awaiting my permission
to make it a
permanent fixture

I close my eyes, unable to finish reading. I know what comes next, but I don't want to read it. I don't even want to write anymore. That poem I wrote six weeks ago sums it up well enough already.

I hate reading what I wrote then. From the outside, I look weak. Pathetic. If I picked up this journal and read it, not knowing the person who wrote it, I'd want to scream at her in frustration. I'd tell her to stand up for herself, that no job or amount of money is worth her dignity.

The trouble is, no matter how loud I scream, I can't seem to hear my own voice.

EIGHT

If I could work seven days a week, I would, but the salon is closed Sundays and Mondays.

Mariah takes Amma to school Monday morning and then drives to work, leaving me stranded at home. It's my day to clean the apartment and do laundry between bouts of schoolwork. Not how I like to spend my time, but necessary.

Get used to it, I think. *You'll be adding diaper changes to the list soon enough.*

I start a load of laundry. When I get back to my room, I notice a missed call from a random number on my phone. As I'm checking my voicemail, someone calls again. I answer it. "This is Everly speaking."

"Hey, Ev."

I recognize the voice immediately. It's Nicolai. "How did you get my number?" I demand.

"Whoa, not even a hello?" He sounds amused.

"Hi." I bite my lip. "How did you get my number?"

"I stole it from Simone's phone."

I smile at the mental image of Nicolai trying to be sneaky. "What do you want?"

"Come to brunch with me." There's a hidden smile in his voice.

"Brunch? It's Monday. Don't you have work?"

"Not yet," he says. "It's still summer. I don't start 'til the beginning of September."

"That's a lame excuse," I tease. "I'm in school, even though it's summer." I'm avoiding answering him, but I glance at the fridge, knowing it's practically empty, and my stomach growls.

"Come on," Nicolai says. "You have to eat either way, so you might as well eat with me. I want to talk to you."

He had me at food, and he's right about us needing to talk. It wasn't fair to leave him at the party after dropping the huge news that I'm pregnant. *After* making out with him and letting things go too far.

"You'll have to pick me up. I don't have a car today." I ignore the fluttering in my stomach, knowing I'm about to see him again.

"Text me your address."

Nicolai's car is nice. He drives a Mercedes C250, and it smells good, clean, like the laundry I should be doing. Normally I like sweet scents, because who wants their surroundings to purposely smell like *chores*? But being pregnant has my senses all screwed up, and the linen air freshener on his air vent is nice.

Nicolai glances at me. I feel the weight of his gaze like something tangible. Heavy. Carrying with it the same anxiety and regret I'm feeling about what happened between us in his room when we saw each other last. Hungry as I am, I feel a wave of regret for agreeing to brunch. He's probably so mad at me for the way I ran out on him. And not only that, but seeing him in person is like a visual reminder of the fact that I can't have him. But I shoo away my emotions and smile. "Where are we eating?" It seems like a safe enough question, all things considered.

"There's a café downtown you'll like."

"You don't know what I like."

He grins. "I know you like Beanbags. And me."

My tongue ties itself in a knot.

I stare out the window the rest of the drive. It doesn't take long for us to arrive. We park in front of a small white Victorian building that looks like a house.

Nicolai puts a few coins in the meter, and he holds the purple-painted door open for me. When we enter the small café, my gaze sweeps over the original paintings for sale hanging above Victorian-style chairs that warmly contrast the burnt-orange walls in the waiting area. The scent of coffee is thick in the air. My stomach growls again.

"This is nice," I comment.

"Wait." Nicolai smirks. "Was that a compliment? As in, you might like this place?"

"That depends. The food might be terrible."

"The food is anything but terrible," he promises.

"You'll be gladly eating those words, as well as whatever you end up ordering."

The hum of voices in the air merges with the clanking of dishes and metal forks scraping on plates. It's not terribly crowded, and we only have to wait briefly before we're seated next to a huge window. Nicolai sits across from me and puts his elbows on the tiny table, and again I'm struck by how attractive he is, how his arms flex with each movement. How symmetrical his face is, with his straight nose and strong jaw. His hair is shiny, and his eyes stand out against his smooth skin like moonbeams.

"What do you eat here?" I ask, glancing at the menu to distract myself from ogling him.

"Usually the eggs Benedict," he says. "Or the breakfast burrito. You can't go wrong with either."

I nod halfheartedly. "What did you want to talk about?" I know damn well already. He's pissed at me for leading him on, twice.

He looks serious and drops his hands to the table. "I like you, Ev."

I wait for more, but he doesn't continue. "That's it?"

"I like you, and I want to get to know you."

Is this guy mental? "Did you not hear the part where I said I was pregnant?"

"Are you and the baby's father in a relationship?"

Me and the baby's father. The idea makes me want to vomit.

I instantly make up my mind to be honest with Nicolai. If anything, scaring him off will be a good thing, since he doesn't seem deterred by the most obvious reason to stay away from me. Whether he means what he says, that he wants to learn more about me, or he's actually hoping for more, he should know how complicated things already are.

"I'm not sure who the baby's dad is. It's definitely between two guys, both of whom I know, but I have no idea which one it is."

I'm not certain what I expect his reaction to be. Surprise maybe? Disgust? But he just nods. The tension radiating over my body slightly loosens.

Then he asks, "What's your plan? If you don't mind telling me. Are you keeping the baby? Are you going to be with whoever the dad is?"

"I don't know the answers to any of those questions, Nick."

"I like when you call me Nicolai," he says. "Everyone else calls me Nick."

I smile a little. "Nicolai." My stomach does a flip as I say it.

"Here's the thing. I like you, though I know I shouldn't. You obviously have a lot going on, and you're my little sister's friend." His eyes are intense. "But I can't help it."

"You barely know me."

"I know. It's weird." He flexes his jaw. "I feel like I do know you, though. Did you know Simone has talked about you to me? I've heard her mention your name before, but I didn't make the connection that you were the hard-working, selfless friend she's talked about. The person who's been taking care of her sister since she was really young, so her mom can work more."

My cheeks burn in embarrassment. I shrug. "It's not

like I chose to do it. When Amma was three, her dad, Chris, left. So my mom pulled me out of school to take care of her."

"How old were you?"

"Fourteen." I jerk my chin up defensively. "But I was mature enough to watch her and teach myself at the same time. Mariah—I mean, my mom—had to work. She refused to become a charity case for Chris's parents, even though they were pretty upset with their son for turning out to be a deadbeat." I glance out the window, watching the wind caress the blades of grass surrounding the parking lot outside. "So I homeschooled myself through high school and worked, a second mom to Amma all the while."

When I shift my gaze back to him, he's searching my face intently. "Simone told me a few other things about you, too," he says. "I thought they were admirable. I can't help but feel like I got a glimpse of the kind of person you are when we were at Beanbags." He narrows his eyes at me from across the table. "You listened to me while I was upset about my mom's affair. You made me feel better. If I'm being honest, it felt like the first time someone saw me in a while." He sighs, staring out the window briefly before returning his gaze to my face. "I feel like we have a connection. There's something between us I can't seem to let go of. I want to know you firsthand. Not just through Simone."

He's exactly the kind of guy I should avoid—the kind who will only complicate this pregnancy mess I'm already in. I don't want to start developing feelings for him. I'd rather just hope John is the father and avoid having any reason not to raise this baby with him. But there's something about Nicolai. He makes me feel lighter somehow. I feel I can tell him anything, and it comforts me, and dammit, my skin tingles every time he comes near me.

"I like you, too." The words slip out before I can stop them. "But this can't happen. There are too many reasons why it shouldn't."

Nicolai tries not to smile and fails.

"What?"

"Nothing. Except I don't see you as someone who follows the rules."

"You're right." I wince. "I'm not and look where it got me."

His smile fades. "Nothing has to happen between us."

I give him a withering look.

"I mean it," he insists. "We can just be friends. All I'm asking is to get to know you better."

"Fine. But what about Simone?"

He considers. "We won't tell her. Since we're just friends, there's no reason to."

Not tell her? I'm about to say there's no way in hell I'm going to secretly finagle with my best friend's brother when I remember there's too much I'm *already* not telling her. "Does she know about your mother's affair?"

"No." He looks guilty, and he should. It's not fair to keep something like that to himself.

"Any plans to fill her in?"

He sighs. "I'm kind of hoping things will blow over, and I won't have to."

"That's dumb, Nicolai."

"Is it?" He gives me a knowing look. "Is what I'm doing any different from you trying to protect Amma from the ugly realities in the world?"

"Fine," I snap. "But you can't keep her in the dark forever. She's bound to catch on sooner or later, and she's going to be pissed at *you* when she realizes you kept it from her."

He purses his lips. I feel sorry for him. It must be traumatizing enough, knowing about his mom's affair, and being the *only* one who knows must be worse.

The only one who knows except me, that is.

My phone chimes. It's Ashton, the salon owner. Normally Willow texts me when it comes to anything work-related, and I'm grateful, because Ashton can be a little intimidating. The only time she's ever contacted me was to tell me I was hired.

I read the message slowly, feeling like I'm about to faint. I read it again to make sure I got it right. A third time, just in case. The message doesn't change.

I need to talk to you ASAP.

The waitress chooses that moment to ask for our orders. Nicolai mutters something, and she leaves. He leans across the table. "You look like you're going to be sick. What's wrong?"

"It's nothing." But I do feel sick. My head is spinning and I grasp the edge of the table with one hand, holding on until the fear recedes.

"I thought we agreed to be friends. You can tell me."

"I—uh, one of the guys who might be the baby's father caught me stealing money at work and has been blackmailing me for sex ever since."

84

Nicolai blinks several times. "Wait a minute. Did you just say he's been *blackmailing* you?"

"Unfortunately, yes." I sigh. "I told him I'm pregnant a few days ago, and he wanted me to have an abortion, but I haven't decided what *I* want to do yet. I won't let him make that choice for me. I think he just told the salon owner I stole the money." I swallow back the burning in my throat.

"What's his name?" His lip seems to curl as he asks the question.

"Vaughn. Why?"

"He's not going to get away with this." His jaw clenches, and the way his eyes harden sets me on edge.

"He will, though. He already has. The damage is done."

The waitress sets plates in front of us. Eggs Benedict and a breakfast burrito. I shoot a surprised look at him. "You ordered for me?"

"You *have* to try them. If you hate them, which I promise you won't, order anything you want."

"Thanks, but I should probably go get fired now. My bosses are waiting to hear from me." I glance at my phone again, but he plucks it from my hand. "Hey!"

He tucks it under his napkin. "They can wait until you—and your baby—have eaten. Please. At least taste both dishes."

He's going to hold my cellphone hostage until I eat? Well … okay then. I *am* hungry, or I was before this conversation. I take a small bite of the breakfast burrito. *Damn. He wasn't lying.* "This is a new level of delicious."

"And now the eggs Benedict."

I cut a piece with the edge of my fork and eat it. Flavors explode into my mouth. "You can have the burrito." I move the plate of eggs in front of me. "This is mine."

"Fair enough." A twinkle dances in his eye.

We stop talking so we can eat, and the painful, hungry ache in my stomach finally disappears. The sad part is, I was starting to get used to the feeling of prolonged hunger.

When he breaks the silence to ask, "Who is the other dad?" it takes me a moment to realize what he's talking about.

I take a long drink of water before answering. "His name is John. Let's just say I really hope he's the father."

"Why?"

I set down my fork. "He wants kids, and not only that, he's wealthy and caring and ... I don't know. Gentle, I guess."

"Gentle?" He laughs. "What do you mean, 'gentle?'"

My face reddens. "Well, Vaughn *isn't* gentle. Not with me. John is different from him in every way."

His smile fades instantly. "Vaughn isn't gentle? Like, he hurts you?"

The last thing I need is for him to get the potential father of my child arrested, so I lie through my teeth. "No, not on purpose. He's just ... passionate, I guess."

He looks disturbed. "Everly—"

"It's fine. I promise."

His hands are balled into fists on the table, and the knuckles are white. He gazes out the window for a while and finally seems to relax. When he looks at me again, his eyes are back to normal. "Do you love him?"

"Vaughn?" Bile rises in my throat. "Of course not."

"No, not him." A flick of a smile comes and goes in the same moment. "John."

"Oh." I'm not sure how to define the way I feel about John. He's safe, whereas Vaughn is dangerous. He's kind and easy to be around. I like him, but I'm not attracted to him. Sadness clings to his every moment, whether life is good or bad. "I care about him as a person," I finally decide. "But I'm not in love with him."

Nicolai nods. "Just wondering."

"Why does it matter?" I kick his foot under the table. "Thought we were just friends."

"I'd rather be your friend than nothing."

It's been a long time since I've had a new friend. After becoming homeschooled, I eventually drifted apart from all my classmates. I couldn't blame them for wanting to fall away from my heavy day-to-day, weighed down with responsibilities that would keep any fun-seeking freshman at bay.

Other than Simone, there's really no one else. Vaughn is the opposite of a friend, and even around John, I'm weighed down by a sense of obligation in case I'm the mother of his child.

"Can I ask you something?" says Nicolai. "If you had family on your dad's side, would you want to meet them?"

I shrug. "I haven't thought about it much. But yeah, probably. Especially since my mom's side refuses to talk about my dad. It would be nice to learn some things about him. Find out what he was like." Nothing to bring me back to reality like talking about that missing piece of my life. "This was great, but I have to go now."

He nods. "Let me drive you. You said you don't have a car."

"Thank you." My shoulders sag in relief. I wasn't going to ask him, but I was secretly hoping he would offer.

He jerks his chin toward the exit. "We pay up there. Let's go." He hands me back my phone, and I check it as we walk to the register. I read another text message while Nicolai pays for our meal. It's from Ashton again.

Meet me at the salon within the hour if you want to keep your job.

NINE

"Wish me luck," I tell Nicolai.

We're parked in the lot behind The Arbor Salon, which is mostly empty because the salon is closed today. The only cars here are Willow's blue Volkswagen Bug, Ashton's Mustang, and—I start—Vaughn's truck.

"Wow," I mutter. "The motherfucker showed up."

"I'll wait here for you." Nicolai turns off the engine. "That way you have a ride home."

The invisible weight on my shoulders feels a little lighter because he only offered to take me to brunch. He probably didn't expect to chauffeur me around all day, but here he is, watching my back. "Thank you, Nicolai. Really." I plant a small kiss on his cheek, and he stiffens. He smells intoxicating, like aftershave and mint, and his long hair tickles my face. I stay close as long as I dare. The way he looks at me sends my stomach into a flurry yet again.

He's Simone's brother, you idiot, I remind myself. *And you're pregnant with another man's child.*

"I'll be right back," I say, my voice thick.

I walk around to the front of the salon and pause before entering. Blood thunders in my ears. I close my eyes and whisper, "I know it's been a while, God, but not getting fired would be really nice. You know, just something to show me you haven't stopped listening to my prayers. Something to show me you still care."

I open the door and go in. Willow is sitting behind the front desk, brow furrowed. "Hi, Everly." She stands. "Follow me." She leads me to the breakroom, where Ashton and Vaughn are sitting at the table, waiting.

I look at Vaughn first. He's wearing a smug smile that makes me want to tackle him to the ground and beat the shit out of him. *Get a grip, Everly. They probably want to talk to us about sales. There's no way Vaughn would rat you out because you might keep the baby.*

Ashton's expression is cold, made more severe by the way her blond hair is pulled away from her face in a topknot. "Everly. Sit down." Willow sits next to her.

I pull a chair out from the table and sit across from the three of them. This feels like an interrogation.

"Vaughn told me you stole money from the register back in June." *That son of a bitch.* "Over a hundred bucks," she adds evenly, no inflection. Her brown eyes pin me in place.

I've never deserved this job. I've never fit in here, with these wealthy people—Ashton, in her designer suit and expensive heels, or Willow with her knack for number crunching and turning anything messy into perfection.

The stylists themselves: talented, pricey, and perfect. Tears trickle down my face before I can stop them.

Ashton and Willow shoot each other a worried glance. "It's true?" Willow asks in disbelief. "You took the money?"

"Yes. I'm so sorry, Ashton." My voice is thick, bordering on hysterical. "I know it's no excuse, but I took it because I'm poor, and I'm pregnant, and we were going to have to go without electricity." My voice is hardly audible, I'm so scared and ashamed. It's embarrassing, breaking down like this in front of them and Vaughn most of all. I didn't want him to see me in this moment of weakness, especially since he's the one who caused it. Bastard.

"Wait a minute," Ashton says, her voice a little softer. "Slow down. You're pregnant?"

I nod. "I'm sorry, Ashton. The register was over, and I really needed it. I'll pay back every penny, even if it takes months."

Willow purses her lips. A deep V appears between her brows.

Vaughn chuckles. "She's hella broke. It will take her longer than a few months, trust me."

Ashton gives him an irritated glance. "You can go," she says dismissively. "Get out, in fact."

Vaughn's smile fades. "Is she gonna get fired?"

"The door is in clear view." Ashton waits for him to leave.

He stands slowly, smirking at me a last time before exiting through the back door. I can't believe he has the nerve to rub his victory in my face like this. I've been at his beck and call for two months, hooking up with him whenever and wherever he asks.

"I got pregnant with my daughter when I was about your age," Ashton says, like it's an explanation.

I try to imagine it. Stylish Ashton, with her perfect blond hair, sharp brown eyes, and tongue like a knife, in a situation even remotely similar to mine.

"It's true," Willow confirms. "We were still in beauty school at the time."

"It was hard," says Ashton. "And the aftermath is even harder. Everyone goes through shit, and the world doesn't care. But I do."

"What?"

"You don't have to pay me back, and you aren't fired. But if you ever steal from this salon again, you will be." Her lips thin. "Also, you're no longer allowed to use the register."

Willow's mouth falls open a little. She seems relieved. Though at which part, I'm not sure. Is she relieved that I'm not fired, or that I'm no longer allowed to use the register?

"Th-thank you." I hold up my hands. "I swear nothing like this will happen again. Thank you so much."

Ashton smiles, nodding. "Go read a pregnancy book or something. God knows I should have."

I hesitate. Now that they know the truth, there's nothing stopping me from telling them Vaughn has been blackmailing me. I could get rid of him right now.

Or … I could hold onto this and show him how it feels. I could hold it over his head, like he's been doing to me. Shift the power balance. At least, until I know if he's the father. And after that? *Good riddance either way, motherfucker!*

I return to the parking lot, where Nicolai is waiting. Vaughn's truck is gone. I get in the car.

"What happened?" he asks. "Are you okay?"

I wipe my face, still wet with tears. "I'm fine."

"Did you get fired?" His eyebrows pinch together with worry. "I can ask my dad if he'll hire you for the landscaping company, maybe put in a good word with a few places—"

I grab Nicolai's shoulders and kiss him. He freezes, just like he did when I kissed him at his welcome home party, and then he snakes his hands through my hair. He deepens the kiss, and I crawl across the middle console into his lap.

He groans, breaking away from my lips to trail kisses down my neck. My body ignites with desire so strong, I can barely see straight. "Nicolai," I murmur, gliding my fingers down his chest.

But he stops me. "You make being your friend really damn hard."

"That's not the only thing I'm making hard."

A grin tugs at his lips. "You're too much."

He's right. This is too much. We shouldn't be doing this. It will only complicate things. But I don't want to resist him. *Blame it on the pregnancy hormones.* "This doesn't have to mean anything." In the back of my mind, I know it's a lie. Or at least, wishful thinking that I know can't possibly end up being true.

His eyes are heavy with desire. I wonder if he sees though the statement, the invitation. "I—" He swallows, appearing to be at a loss for words. I wait for him to answer, anticipation thrumming in my veins.

But before he can say another word, the car door opens, and someone pulls me out and drags me away from him.

A second later I'm thrown on the ground, and I hear shouting. "That's my girl, bro! What the hell do you think you're doing?"

Nicolai gets out of the car and stares the guy down. "I take it you must be Vaughn?"

"That's right!" He throws his hands up.

I stare in horror as Nicolai nods once before punching him square in the face. Immediately, Vaughn falls to the ground, landing on his side.

I get to my feet and run over to Vaughn to make sure he didn't hit his head. Luckily, he didn't land on it and he's still breathing. My gaze jumps to Nicolai. He's watching me with narrowed brows. "What the hell is wrong with you? Why did you do that?"

"Are you kidding?" he asks, bewildered.

I know his confusion is warranted. I hate Vaughn with every fiber of my being, but if he's potentially the father of my child, I'd really prefer for him to be alive. Just like I'd prefer that my own father was alive.

"Just go," I tell him, suddenly drained. "I'll find another ride home."

"Wait, Everly. Please." He moves toward me, but I glare at him.

"Leave me alone, Nicolai. I mean it." I don't know why I'm so angry. I feel like I might break at any moment. I'm upset that Nicolai had to defend me in the first place, that the situation I'm in has become my life.

"He threw you on the ground, Ev!" He grabs a fistful of his hair in frustration. "You can be mad at me if you want, but that's not okay. And you're *pregnant*."

The words prick me like a needle.

Pregnant. That's right. I'm pregnant. And Vaughn threw me on the ground.

The shock of it is almost too much. I sink to my knees, a sob building in my throat.

He lifts me back up. "Come on," he pleads. "Just let me take you home."

I nod, unable to think straight. What is wrong with me? Why do I keep defending Vaughn after everything he's done? Is it hormones, insecurity, or just a natural instinct to prevent conflict? Either way, I'm more annoyed at myself than I want to admit.

We get in Nicolai's car and drive off.

I stare out the window, unseeing. "I'm sorry," I whisper. "It's just that—"

"I know," he says. "Don't apologize." He's gripping the steering wheel hard, but when his eyes meet mine, they're gentle. Gentle, like John's. "There's nothing a person won't do for family," he states.

I grimace. "Vaughn isn't family."

"Not yet," he says darkly. "But he might be."

The rest of the car ride is spent in uncomfortable silence. I'm more than a little ashamed of the way I reacted to Nicolai defending me. Even if my first instinct was to defend Vaughn, I shouldn't have. The way he's treated me is inexcusable.

Nicolai keeps the engine running when he stops in front of the apartment. The last thing I want to do is say goodbye, but it's probably for the best. I need time to think and gather my emotions.

"Again, thank you for everything," I say as I get out of the car. "I'm sorry for getting mad at you. I think I'm just hormonal."

He laughs. "Really, Ev, it's fine. You have nothing to apologize for." His smile and gaze linger on me as I shut the door. He lifts his fingers from the steering wheel in a salute-wave and drives away.

As soon as I'm in my room, I take out my notebook and steady myself with a deep breath. It's time to finish reading that last entry. I need to remember why I should hate Vaughn. I need to remind myself why I should never defend him again.

I pick back up in the middle of the page, just after Mariah dropped me off at his house.

You should have known something was up. When Vaughn answered the door, his dark gaze lingered on you a moment too long. He flung the front door open wider and allowed you inside.

"What do you want?" you said, crossing your arms while you stepped inside.

"You came."

"Clearly. Why did you make me?"

"Because I want you again," he said.

Ugh. Everly, your stomach churned. Somehow you knew he was going to say that, but stupidly, you hoped you were wrong. "Is anyone else here?"

"No. My parents are at work."

You asked, "You live with your parents? How old are you again?"

He cocked an eyebrow. "I'm nineteen. Don't worry, they won't be home for a long time."

If his words were meant to comfort you, they did the opposite. "What makes you think this is going to be a regular thing? The agreement was supposed to be one hookup in exchange for your silence. Let's leave it at that."

His expression was enough to send chills up your spine. "One time isn't enough. By now I hope you've realized you can't make me stay quiet unless you do what I want."

He kissed your neck and fumbled at the buttons on your jeans. You considered pushing him away, Everly. In that moment, you wanted to tell Willow what you did, just to see that triumphant look fall from his face. Make it all stop.

But there's just no way you can do that. Your job is a godsend. You need it, especially now.

So you told yourself if you closed your eyes and pretended to be somewhere else, you might be able to forget where you were and who you were with.

You pushed your pants down, and he eagerly removed your shirt. He finished undressing before you could blink and threw you stomach-down on the sofa.

And then you remembered how you felt last time, yelling, "Wait! You need to wear a condom. I'm not on birth control." You weren't about to make the same mistake twice.

He nodded and ran upstairs. When he returned, you twisted your head so you could see he'd taken your advice.

Oh, Everly. This next part is really hard to write about, but you're afraid if you don't, bottling it up inside might actually kill you.

Vaughn grabbed your hair and shoved your face into the cushion. You could hardly breathe, and the rough fabric scratched as it slid back and forth across your face. It was a welcome distraction, but not good enough.

So you imagined you were at a car dealership, test-driving a new convertible. Remember when you were a child, and Grandpa would take you to the dealership and pretend to be shopping for a new car? He always let you pick out any car in the lot and you'd test drive it together. Then when you got back, he'd pretend not to like the car for some fake reason so he wouldn't have to buy it, when really you guys just didn't have any money. Even though you never got to take home any of the cars after test-driving them, you learned a lot about the cars and grew to love them. They made you happy, and so did the memories of driving around town with your cackling Grandpa.

Maybe that's why, pinned underneath Vaughn, you thought about the smell of fresh leather and fabric spray. Maybe that's why you drummed up the feeling of hot leather seats against the backs of bare thighs in your denim shorts.

The top was down, and a cool breeze blew into your face and lifted your curls.

You ran the vision on a loop in your mind, Everly, expecting it to bring you peace. But you couldn't quite get there.

Here, in the real world, there's only pain. Only violation.

When he finished, he lay on top of you, his dead weight trapping you.

"I'm test-driving a convertible," you thought. "There's wind in my hair and the leather seats are hot against the backs of my thighs. I'll drive and drive until I leave everything else behind."

I clamp my jaw shut against the panic. Why did I read

this? What was I thinking? As if it wasn't traumatic enough going through it the first time.

"Relax," I whisper to myself. "*Relax*, dammit. He has no hold over you now. Willow and Ashton know the truth, and you didn't get fired. It's *over*."

The breath I blow out of my mouth is long, necessary, and takes with it the worries and trauma that have crushed me for the past six weeks.

Now all I have to do is figure out how to stay standing until I know for sure who my baby's father is.

TEN

"Can we do something fun today?" Amma pouts, making her eyes look big and round. "We never get to do anything fun." She sets her backpack down on the seat next to her in the back of the car. The school parking lot is packed with cars, so we're stuck sitting here until things start to clear up.

"Amma …" I don't know what to tell her. I agree with her that we never get to do anything fun. But how do I tell a little kid that it's because we're always broke without worrying or depressing her?

It's like she can read my mind. "It doesn't have to be something that costs money." She gives me a serious look from the backseat. "It can be free and still fun."

I sigh. "I guess that's true. Mom's not off work 'til later tonight anyway."

She beams. "Exactly!"

I laugh at her enthusiasm. "What do you want to do?"

We're quiet while she thinks. The car in front of me

starts to move forward, so I ease off the brake and idle forward, careful of the kids walking in the gaps between cars.

"Let's paint flowers on rocks and take them to the cemetery!"

I frown. That was probably the last thing I expected her to say. "Why?"

"So the graves without any flowers on them won't be empty anymore," she says matter-of-factly.

I meet her eyes through the rearview mirror. My throat burns with the emotion I'm trying to suppress. "I think that's a really good idea, Amma."

An hour later, we're driving to the cemetery, which is right off the road near an older shopping center in town. An assortment of river rocks is nestled in Amma's old Easter basket, which she's holding proudly on her lap in the backseat.

We park and take a walking path lined with tall, shady trees, carrying our basket to the first bare expanse of graves we see. Amma arranges her flower-painted rocks in patterns; yellow, orange, pink, white. Yellow, orange, pink, white. Happy colors, she calls them.

Then I notice a familiar face. It's the last face I expect to see here. Nicolai is setting three bouquets of yellow daisies on a grave, his expression solemn. What the hell is he doing here?

"Amma, I'm going to see if I can find more empty graves. Be right back."

She nods without looking up. She's still arranging some stones in her favorite pattern.

I walk to where Nicolai is paying his respects, but he doesn't notice. Not until I say, "Fancy seeing you here."

His gaze jumps to mine. "Everly?"

I jerk my chin toward the tombstone he's standing at. "Who are you visiting?" And then I read the name. *Cindy Turner.* "Is this a family member of yours?"

He smiles faintly. "My birth mom. She died when I was twelve."

"Your birth mother?" My brain is a haze of confusion. "You're adopted?"

He nods. "I thought you knew that."

"I knew Simone was," I say. "But for some reason I thought you were Mr. and Mrs. Beckett's biological son."

"Ah." He shoves his hands in his pockets. "Well, you're not too far off. My mom is my birth mother's older sister. My aunt, by blood. But I was placed in her care as a baby, so I've always considered her my mother."

"That explains the uncanny resemblance." I try to sound upbeat.

He chuckles. "Yeah." Staring past me, he catches sight of Amma. "Is that the famous younger sister?"

"Yeah. She wanted to paint flowers on rocks and bring them to the empty graves."

He blinks. "Wow. That's really sweet."

"I know. Told you she's a nut job."

A shadow of a smile lingers on his lips. "I'll let you get back."

I remain in front of him, even though I know I'm supposed to walk away now. But I don't want to. "You want a rock?" I ask.

"What?"

"A rock," I repeat. "With a flower painted on it. For your birth mother's grave?"

He searches my face. I'm not sure what he finds there, but whatever it is makes his next words sound tender. "Thanks. That would be nice."

"Okay." Over my shoulder, I call for Amma. "This guy needs a rock!" I yell.

Amma comes over with her basket. She quizzically looks up at Nicolai. "Who are you?"

"This is my friend, Nicolai. You remember Simone, right?" I ask her. She nods. "Well, this is Simone's brother."

"Oh." She grins. "I'm Amethyst, but you're allowed to call me Amma."

Nicolai laughs. "Thanks. I feel very honored."

"Do you need a flower?" She sounds eager, excited. Like her services being requested have given her a new purpose.

"I sure do," he tells her. He motions to the bouquets of fresh daisies he brought. "You see, I heard about your painted rocks, and I'm afraid the flowers I bought are nothing in comparison."

"Okay." Amma nods seriously, her brows furrowed in concentration. "Let me see what I got." She picks up a few rocks, nudging several to the side until she finds a massive one at the bottom. There's a pink rose painted on it. "This is the best one. I was saving it for last, but I think you should take it."

She puts it in Nicolai's hand. He's smiling politely, but I notice his Adam's apple bob when he swallows. "This means a lot to me, Amma." He kneels down and scoots

104

his flowers off to the side, placing the rock right in the center.

"We better get going," I say. "My mom gets off work soon."

"See you around." Nicolai stands up and glances at my lips. I feel his gaze travel straight to my knees.

"I hope so," I say quietly.

Amma waves. "Bye, Nicolai."

He waves back, his smile back in place for her. "Bye."

When we get in the car, Amma says, "He's really nice."

"You have no idea," I mutter.

I drive across town to Mariah's work. She's sitting on the curb outside with her chin resting in her hands. To her left sits her manager, talking incessantly though she's clearly paying him no notice.

As soon as she sees us waiting, she perks up and stands. "See you tomorrow, Kirk." She eagerly gets in the car. "Thank God, mija."

I laugh. "Kirk really doesn't seem that bad. Maybe you should give him a chance."

"Not funny." She swats me playfully. "Never. Suggest it again and you're grounded."

I snort. "What does *grounded* mean?"

"Remind me again why I let you talk to me like this." She checks her appearance in the mirror and wipes a sheen of sweat from her forehead.

"Because you're young enough to be my sister."

"Fair enough." She turns to Amma in the backseat. "Hi love-bug."

"Hi, Mommy." Amma holds up her Easter basket. "Everly took me to the graveyard today."

Mariah turns her puzzled grin onto me. "Sounds … lively."

I tell her all about the rocks as I drive us home. She laughs when I mention the pattern Amma insisted on forming the rocks into.

"I have the sweetest girls in the world," she says. It's always somewhat jarring when she refers to me as her child, because I rarely feel like one. I try not to let it bother me that Mariah is so much more motherly with Amma than me, because the fact of the matter is she was a child when she had me. With Amma, she was an adult.

We get out of the car at home. As I'm walking up the stairs to the apartment, I spot Vaughn's truck in the guest parking. *No. There's no reason for him to come here.*

I ignore it, hoping he'll drive away when he sees I'm with my mother and sister. I lock the door behind us and my mom starts up the stove to make dinner.

"I'm going to my room to lie down," I tell Mariah. It's been a long day, and pregnancy is making me tired. I shuffle down the hall to my room and fall dramatically onto my bed. My comforter has never felt so good. Sleep has never sounded so appealing. I close my eyes. I'm about to nod off when the doorbell rings.

I try not to worry. I doubt Vaughn will ask for me when Mariah answers the door. He'll probably say he got the wrong address and wait until tomorrow at work to tell me whatever he has to say.

My bedroom door opens. "There's someone here to see you, mija," Mariah says. "Someone named Vaughn?"

My stomach clenches. I can't believe he actually asked for me. Must he poison every moment of my life with his presence, even my days off?

"It's probably about church choir," I lie. No need to clue her in to what's happening in my life—or my body—just yet. That can wait until I know whose DNA my baby shares. Besides, all I'll have to do to get rid of him is threaten to report him for blackmailing me. I'm the one with the upper hand now that the truth about the money is out.

She gives me a stern look. "I'm going to make dinner. Be smart, Everly."

Be smart. If only she knew exactly how smart I have suddenly become. She leaves and is replaced by Vaughn, who looks pleased with himself. "Hey, babe."

"What the hell are you thinking, coming here?" I scowl. "Go away!"

"Want to go on a date?"

"You can't be serious. After what you pulled, telling Ashton I stole the money and throwing me on the ground, I never want to see you again!"

He chuckles. "Bet you wish you'd listened to me. If you'd gotten rid of the baby, you wouldn't have forced me to tell on you. You'd still have a job."

Though the words sting, my laughter has a nasty edge to it. "I do still have a job. Ashton didn't fire me. You're a dumbass with no cards left to play."

Silence. Glorious, shocked silence, and I revel in every precious second of it.

"Are you fucking kidding me?" His face becomes red.

"Not even a little bit. Screw you, Vaughn." It feels

good to gloat, but I'm painfully aware that if he ends up being the father of my child, my victory will be short-lived.

He blinks away his irritation. "That's too bad, but I guess it doesn't matter. Now stop playing hard to get and let me take you out."

"Absolutely not."

"Fine," he says. "You're already in bed. At least now I don't have to work for it."

"Don't touch me." I cross my arms. "If you so much as take one more step, I'll report you for blackmail and sexual assault."

A slow smile creeps onto his face, making my stomach churn. "You haven't told your mom about me yet, have you? Or the baby?" He takes my terrified silence for an answer and continues, "Wouldn't it be a shame if she learned about our predicament? I'm guessing she doesn't know about John, either. I can tell her if you want."

I stare past him, expressionless. "When did you become so charming?"

He chuckles and climbs onto the bed. He straddles me, reaching for my shirt. My mind is spinning like a wheel as I try to think quickly through my panic. Mariah will find out eventually, so I could just call his bluff. But if he tells her that I don't know who the father is, I know it will break her heart. It will make Amma look down on me —her second mother figure.

What could possibly derail him from the act that drives his every thought?

"Just so you know," I say hopefully, "I've been spotting. That means bleeding." I pause. "It's heavy."

He wrinkles his nose. "Gross."

I nod. "Yep."

His mouth turns down in a scowl. "Can't you put a tampon in or some shit?"

I stare at him blankly. Did he really just ask me that? "It doesn't really work that way, Vaughn."

He rolls off me and straightens his clothes. "Fine. I gotta go. You win this time." He eyes me one more time, like I'm a cake he was told he can't eat 'til after dinner, and then leaves.

I fall back on the bed, my relief palpable. *Don't question it, Everly, just let it be.* But no matter how hard I try, my mind is like an endlessly spinning wheel. I fetch my notebook and write:

Dear Everly.

Why is Vaughn afraid of a little blood?

It's ironic, considering the pain he inflicts on you every time you're forced to feel his skin against yours. The hole he's creating in your heart isn't only bleeding, but scarring.

A scarring hole is worse than a bleeding one because a bleeding hole still gives you hope. It has the potential to heal, to close up nicely, leaving no evidence of today's pain behind. But a scarring hole leaves with it a reminder of who created the hole in the first place.

As far as you're concerned, Vaughn's hands are covered in blood. He has no reason to be afraid.

ELEVEN

Sometimes it feels like I live my life in a constant state of lying.

It's been a week since I bumped into Nicolai at the cemetery, and we haven't spoken since. But today, I decide to call him for the first time and ask him to—wait for it— lie for me!

When he answers after a few rings, I sound way too enthusiastic. "Nicolai!" *Too much. Tone it down a notch. Fuck.* "What are you doing today?" I ask, not as loudly this time.

A pause. "Nothing, why?"

"It's just ..." I close my eyes. This was a bad idea. A *terrible* idea. It's bad enough I didn't tell John or Vaughn that my first OBGYN appointment is today. What I'm about to ask of Nicolai is even worse, especially after the way I treated him, yelling at him to leave me alone when he punched Vaughn.

I shouldn't continue leading him on when nothing,

nothing, can happen between us. Not while my life is a mess. Not with us lying to Simone, hiding from her the time we've spent together. We've had two sleepovers this week, giving me plenty of opportunities to tell her. I know there's a chance she would be okay with it, but when it comes down to it, I'm still pregnant with another man's child.

"The thing is, I need a ride to my ultrasound appointment in twenty minutes, and I was wondering if you'd be available to take me. But if not it's fine. *Totally* fine. I can take a taxi or something."

Nicolai laughs. "Ev, relax. That's what friends do, right? I'll be right there." He hangs up, and I stare at the phone, relieved.

I couldn't bear to tell the dads about the appointment. If they'd both wanted to come, and I had to watch my doctor's expression become fixed into a permanent state of judgment, I'd have died a little inside.

Besides, inviting John would mean inviting Vaughn. He's got as much a shot at being the father as John does, but he's the last person on earth I want to see.

I get ready quickly, brushing my teeth and braiding my hair. I dress in shorts and a white V-neck. When Nicolai texts me that he's here, I rush outside.

"Thanks again for driving me," I say when I get in. I face him, noting the scent of his smooth aftershave, the way his bun accentuates the lines of his jaw and neck. His blue shirt brings out his eyes more than ever.

"No problem." He looks me over slowly, too, and then blinks, seeming to catch himself, and turns away.

But the damage is already done. His look starts a burn

in my veins. I clench my hands into fists to keep from grabbing and kissing him, like I did a week ago.

Just friends, Everly. Just friends.

"There's something else I wanted to ask you too," I say. "And if you say no, I won't be offended."

"Say no? To you?" Nicolai arches a brow. "I'm *very* curious, now. What is it?"

I bite away my forming smile and spit out what I'm trying to say. "It's just that I'm in the worst possible predicament. You know, without knowing who the father is. It's only a matter of time until my doctor finds out and starts judging me." I swallow. "So I was hoping if she saw me with an attractive, stable guy first, while getting to know me, her first impression of me wouldn't be based on the fact that I don't know who my baby's dad is." I know it's a stupid concern to have, considering all my other problems, but dammit, it still bothers me.

Nicolai grins. "Me being the attractive, stable guy?" He points to himself with his thumb.

I can tell he's pleased. "Yes."

He glances at me. "You want me to pretend to be the father of your child?"

It sounds ridiculous even to me. "I know it's a lot to ask. I promise I won't be offended if you don't want to—"

"Everly, please," he cuts me off, a smile in his voice. "I'm not offended. I'm honored, in fact, that you'd choose me to be the fake daddy of your baby."

"Honored?" I laugh. "Really?"

He shrugs. "Well, yeah. I mean, look at you. I'd have to be a total stud for someone like you to let me procreate with them."

My cheeks burn furiously, surely making my face match my hair. "You're way too nice to me, Nico."

A funny expression crosses his face. "Nico? I like that. No one's ever called me that before."

"Well, you seemed to take offense to Nick, so I had to come up with something."

We're at a stoplight now, and out the window, I watch a mother pushing her baby around in a stroller down the sidewalk. The sun is bright, right in the child's eyes. The mom reaches under the stroller for a blanket, draping it over the top of the stroller for extra shade.

"Turn right here," I tell him, since he doesn't know where he's going, and I change the subject. "How did you get a scholarship for college?"

"Football," he answers.

I shoot an amused glance at him. "I should have known."

"Known what?"

"That you played football. It's written all over you."

He blushes. "Is that a bad thing?"

I gaze at his arms, toned and strong, his tan skin and thick legs. "No."

He laughs. "All right then."

"You don't know how lucky you are to have a talent like that to get you into college for free." I can't hide the bitterness in my tone. I hope he doesn't notice.

He purses his lips. "I guess I am." His attention flickers to me. "What about you? What's on the ambitious Everly's college agenda?"

"I've been in college for a year, and I'm taking

summer classes online right now. School is where I met your sister."

"What are you majoring in?" he asks.

"Engineering, I think. Unless you know of something better that will ensure I make lots of money."

"Money is that important to you then?" His eyes narrow.

"Yeah. It is. When you don't have it, you learn what a necessity it is. A lot of people don't think of themselves as rich, but they can buy food for their families, put gas in their cars, and pay for a roof over their heads without wondering when it will happen again. That's rich."

He's silent for a long moment before he says, "I guess that's true. And family. Family is another valuable thing people take for granted."

"Definitely. I want to do everything I can to make sure I don't struggle the way my mom always has for her family. She chose us over money, but I want both."

"You can have that," he says. "I believe in you. You already have a head start on the family part." He looks pointedly at my stomach, earning a glare from me.

"We'll see."

"I'm surprised your mom never tried to track down your dad's family," Nicolai says. "I bet they would have helped her out with money. You're their blood, after all."

"She did, but there wasn't really social media when she was in high school," I tell him. "And even now, Jones is such a common last name that it would be impossible to nail someone down."

He shrugs. "Maybe she didn't try hard enough."

Talking about this is pointless. Anything regarding my dad or his family will only lead to false hope. The idea of meeting them and learning more about him is too happy a possibility to fathom. It's too good to be true. I don't want to get my hopes up. "Let me know if you find anything on Mariah Martin's late one-night stand, Leland Jones."

We park in the lot of my doctor's office, surrounded by a cluster of white one-story buildings. Nicolai takes my hand, threading his fingers through mine. I shoot him an incredulous look.

"If you want her to think we're having a baby together," he says, a tantalizing grin on his lips, "then we need to be convincing."

I don't have time to form a response because we're walking through the entrance. The staff beams at us from the counter. My shoes squeak as I cross the shiny white floor to grab a clipboard of paperwork, and we find seats in the waiting room with two other couples.

One of the couples is older, probably in their mid to late thirties, and the other looks to be in their twenties.

Great. We're the youngest ones here.

I fill out the paperwork, and then the older couple is called in, leaving us alone with the younger one.

"How far along are you?" the girl asks. She's white, with a blunt blond bob. Her belly is large and round. She looks ready to pop.

"I'm not sure yet," I say. "This is my first appointment."

"Ooh, exciting!"

Nicolai leans forward. "It really is. I can't wait to be a dad."

I elbow him to keep him from laying it on too thick, but he shrugs innocently.

The girl smiles. "We're excited too. Dan has always wanted a daughter, so we were thrilled when we found out we're having a girl."

Dan wordlessly flips the page of his magazine.

"What are you hoping for?" she asks.

I scrunch my nose. This lady is a little too much for me. I'm about to tell her I don't really give a damn when Nicolai cuts in. "We're hoping for healthy," he says pleasantly.

She smiles, melting a little at his answer. I resist the urge to laugh or smack him. He's way too good at this and maybe even having fun with it.

"Have you picked out any names?" she asks. "We're naming her Veronica after me."

"Oh, yeah, we have plenty." Nicolai puts an arm around my shoulder. "But our top contenders are Ellie for a girl and Nolan for a boy."

Ellie and Nolan? As much as I hate to admit it, dammit, I kinda like the names.

"Everly?" a nurse pokes her head inside the waiting room. "Come on back."

Nicolai stands with me, and I offer a parting smile to Veronica and her indifferent partner.

The nurse takes me to an alcove with a scale nestled within to check my weight. I step on the scale and am surprised to find I weigh the same as I normally do. We're then ushered into a room and told the doctor will be with us shortly.

"Nolan and Ellie?" I ask as soon as we're alone.

"Those are my baby names." He smirks. "You better not steal them."

"I haven't even thought about names yet, so don't worry."

"Really?" He frowns. "Don't girls love making lists of baby names? Picking them out way ahead of time?"

"Maybe, but not me. I wasn't sure if I even wanted kids." I'm still not, but it's too late now.

The doctor knocks and comes in. "Everly, hi. I'm Dr. Norman." She shakes my hand. "And is this …?"

"This is Nicolai," I say. "The baby's father."

She nods and shakes his hand, and he oozes charm all over the place.

A pang shoots through me when it strikes me how much I wish my pregnancy was as simple, as easy, as this. I wish this could have happened with someone like Nicolai. Not someone nearly twice my age, or someone I despise. And seeing Nicolai perform here seems to shock the reality into me that this is not my situation. It feels like he's showing me what I could have had if things had gone differently. I try to keep a smile in place as he takes my hand, as he gazes at me with adoration. As he says things any pregnant woman would want to hear. I try to smile, when really, each gesture feels like a personal blow.

This is the reason you asked him to do this, Everly, I think. *And he's doing a damn good job.*

"Okay, let's take a look and see what's going on in there," says Dr. Norman. She makes me lie down and has Nicolai stand near my head. I raise my shirt and she squirts warm gel on my stomach, then smears it with a handheld device and moves it around until she's satisfied.

"And there's your baby," Dr. Norman says, pointing to a screen.

I squint at the blob she's referring to, waiting for that magical moment I've seen in movies to hit me. But it just looks like a blob to me. So, I paste on a fake smile for Nicolai and the doctor's benefit.

"You're measuring at seven weeks and three days gestation."

"Cool," I say. "I have a question about that actually." Since my act can only last so long, this is as good an opportunity as any to test the waters. See how the doctor will react to my situation if she thinks I'm talking about someone else. "My best friend is pregnant too, but she's not sure who her baby's dad is," I say. "She was wondering at what point she can get a DNA test done but was too embarrassed to ask her doctor, so I told her I'd ask you."

Dr. Norman nods. She seems to buy my story. "There are a couple options. She can wait until the second trimester to have testing done, but there is a small chance of miscarriage or harming the baby, as a needle is inserted into the stomach to draw out and test a small amount of amniotic fluid. The other option is non-invasive and can be done as early as seven weeks."

I raise my eyebrows. I'm almost into my third month already. "Really? Seven weeks?"

"Yes. All we'd need is a blood draw from the mother and a cheek swab from the fathers. Results take about a week to come back. The only downside with that option is the cost. It's pricey, around $1500 to $2000, depending on area and insurance."

My stomach sinks. *Two thousand dollars?* "Are there any other options?"

"Wait until the baby is born and have a test done after that. Do you have any other questions?"

My shoulders sag. "No."

"Then go ahead and get yourself cleaned up," she says. "I'll see you in a few weeks."

Since getting in the car, Nicolai hasn't spoken a word. It's like he knows my brain is a whirlwind of chaos.

Harmful to the baby. Miscarriage. Non-invasive. Pricey. Wait until the baby is born.

I look at the photo of my little blob, printed out for me before I left.

What the hell am I supposed to do?

It's killing me, not knowing if the baby's father is Vaughn or John. Though I've been hoping for a miscarriage since finding out I was pregnant, this photo is making me think twice. A needle in my stomach sounds painful, and there's no way I can afford to have the non-invasive testing done instead.

"What are you going to do?" Nicolai asks.

"I don't know," I mutter. "Wait, I guess?"

"Why not have the testing done?"

"Didn't you hear how much it costs?" I laugh humorlessly. "I don't have that kind of money."

"Yeah, but ..." he pauses, "John does, from what you've told me. Why not ask him? I'm sure he'd be willing, if it meant finding out if the kid is his or not."

I shake my head. "The only thing worse than not having money is asking someone else for it. Not to mention, I wouldn't want John to feel like he wasted his money if the baby turns out to be Vaughn's."

He purses his lips. "You'll never know unless you ask him."

We park outside my apartment complex. Several kids are sitting on the sidewalk in front, taking selfies and laughing as they look over the pictures.

I should probably get out of the car, but I'm not ready to face the reality of my shitty life just yet. Being around Nicolai makes me forget what it's like to be me. "Thank you for today, Nico."

"Anytime, Ev." He sounds like he means it.

I can't let him become a part of my messy life. He deserves better than that. He deserves better than me.

"Really, though." I fight the knot in my throat. "I have to stop dragging you into my shit."

He looks surprised. "If it means spending time with you ..." He glances at my lips. "Drag me through hell."

"You don't mean that." I don't know if I'm trying to convince him or myself. I've had enough disappointment in my life. I don't know if I can handle Nicolai being another one.

"Yes, I do." He touches my cheek, lighting a fire on my skin like a match to a newspaper. He leans toward me and grazes my forehead with his lips.

The gesture is sweet, making the knot in my throat thicken. He must know the effect he has on me, after I've twice shown I can hardly keep my hands off him. He hasn't asked for anything more, though. It's almost as if he really is satisfied with being my friend.

When I get inside, I'm going to have to write:

Dear Everly,
    He's like a magnet
    attracting the negative because
    he's so positive.
    He latches onto all the bad inside you,
    pulling it out,
    taking it away.
    Where does he take it?
    You don't know.
    But it's
    gone,
    gone,
    gone,
    until he is, too.

"Bye, Nicolai," I say, half in a daze as I get out of the car. Time to return to counting pennies. Time to help my mom pay the bills and do laundry, finish my homework, help Amma with hers, and make dinner. Time to ignore Cupid's arrow in my ass, signed with Nicolai's name in cursive.

TWELVE

"Let's go to the beach." Simone sips her coffee discreetly and then tucks it back under the front desk when a client walks up. She rings him up, schedules his next appointment, and turns back to me. "We're off in an hour and it's perfect outside."

"I don't know," I say. "I should go home. I have school tonight." We've been working all morning, and her offer sounds more than a little tempting. But I've been distracted lately, and I'm worried I haven't been focusing enough on school. The smart thing to do would be going home and studying.

"Oh, come on," she pleads. "It will be nice. Pick your sister up and drop her off for a playdate or something. You need a break. Plus, we haven't hung out in forever. You're going to have a big belly soon and then you'll have to start being more careful with yourself."

She makes a good case. Simone and I used to go out almost every weekend last semester. Now it feels like I only see her at work. With my mind on this pregnancy, finding out who helped cause it, and getting through school I haven't had time for much of anything else. "Only if you drive. That way I can read my book for class in the car." I eye my paperback copy of *Oedipus the King*, required reading for my literature class. Ironically, I enjoy it more than the engineering class I've been trudging painfully through.

She claps her hands. "Yay! You're the best!" She throws her arms around me, squeezing tightly.

I laugh. "I know."

The rest of the shift passes quickly with the knowledge that we'll soon be under the sun, the ocean surrounding us and the sand squishing between our toes. I stop at home to change first. I layer a pink dress over the bikini I put on, which squeezes tightly, painfully over my growing breasts. At least my stomach is still flat, because I don't even own a one-piece to hide it.

I toss a towel, some sunscreen, and an extra change of clothes into a bag before driving to Amma's school.

She knows something's up as soon as she's in the car. "You're going somewhere fun without me, aren't you?"

"I'm sorry. I really am."

She crosses her arms. "Not fair. I want to come."

"It's not so bad. I called Jaycee's mom before I got here and she heated up her hot tub for you guys!"

Amma's stony expression cracks. "Will you at least tell me where you're going?"

"The beach with Simone." I wave my hand at her. "Boring stuff, really. I'll be reading school-books the entire time."

She wrinkles her nose. "That does sound boring. Okay, take me to Jaycee's!"

I grin. "Right away, miss."

"You ready?" I ask when Simone opens the door. She's wearing denim shorts over a purple one-piece swimsuit. Sunglasses are perched atop her head, and her hair is up in a bun. "Almost. Just waiting on Nick. I'm so excited. I've been wanting to go to the beach all summer!"

But I'm stuck on the word she just said. Or the name, rather. "Nick?"

"Oh, yeah," she says brightly. "I invited my brother to come along. I hope you don't mind."

"Not—not at all." Maybe if I pretend to be nauseous, she'll let me go home before Nicolai sees me. It's one thing to spend time with him alone, but it's another to interact with him around Simone and pretend to be mere acquaintances.

He comes down the stairs, clad in some black swim trunks and sandals. And ... that's it. He's not wearing a shirt, but holding one, along with a bottle of sunscreen. His skin is shiny, like he just finished applying it.

"You okay, Ever?" Simone elbows me.

I blink, breaking my stare. "Fine. Just fine." But I'm not. Seeing him has my stomach tying itself in knots.

"Everly, right?" Nicolai says, meeting my gaze. "I remember you from the party."

Gratitude washes over me. He's going to keep the facade going. I know this is the perfect opportunity to come clean—tell Simone everything that's happened between me and Nicolai. But why open that can of worms when I'm still hoping John is the father of this baby? If he is, I'll have the perfect co-parent. I'll have every reason to raise my child with him.

I play along with Nicolai's charade, feigning confusion. "Was it the party that we met at? I forgot."

His mouth twitches. "I believe so."

"Put your shirt on and let's go," Simone tells him. "I don't want to wait too long or we're gonna hit traffic."

"My sunscreen is still drying." He fans his bare chest with the white T-shirt he's holding.

"Ugh. Fine." Simone checks her phone. "I'm going to get the AC going in the car." She turns to me. "Coming?"

"I'm going to use the restroom first if that's okay." I point down the hall.

"Okay, sure. See you in a minute." Simone goes out the front door, leaving Nicolai and I alone, still facing one another.

Slowly, his eyes travel up my body. "You look beautiful."

I blush. "Who are you again?"

He smiles faintly, but it doesn't reach his eyes. "I'm your friend's brother." The way he says it sounds bitter. Regretful.

My lips thin. "We should probably get going."

"Right behind you."

We walk out the front door and Simone has the car running, music blaring as she applies lipstick. "Come on, guys," she calls through the open window.

Nicolai offers me the front seat, and I gratefully take

it. As we drive, the music stays loud, and I eventually give up on trying to read, singing along with Simone to every song that plays. We laugh, letting the wind blow our hair around through the rolled-down windows. Nicolai doesn't say much, but at one point, we make eye contact through the side mirror. His eyes burn back at me, dark around the edges. Unnamed emotions that I don't want to unpack simmer in his expression. My brain goes blank, and I stumble over the words of the song. But then he smiles, and breaks eye contact, looking out the window.

When we get to the beach, Simone swears. "I forgot a water bottle."

I search my bag to see if I brought one. But I, too, left mine at home. "I don't have one either. Sorry."

Nicolai gets out of the car. "Don't worry. I'm sure we can grab some from the boardwalk." He opens my door and reaches to help me out.

My cheeks burn, but I take his hand anyway. Not taking it would only be more suspicious. His face is a mask of kind indifference, on par with the way a friend's brother would look at his sister's friend. When I turn to grab the book I had set on the center console, I almost choke as his hand gently brushes my hip. Swallowing hard I straighten and turn. "Thanks." He gives me a knowing look, like he sees what that careless touch did to me. I glance nervously at Simone but she's staring at her phone, completely unaware of anything.

The beach is busy as we make our way to the sand and find a place to lay out. The hot California sun makes sweat drip down my shoulder blades as I help Simone spread the beach towels out on the soft, fine sand. We use our bags to hold the corners down against the warm wind. A flock of seagulls call as they surround a group with sandwiches a few feet away. One of the girls stands and unsuccessfully tries to shoo them away with her hand.

"Nick, can you go get us some water bottles?" Simone asks.

"Yeah, sure." He gets up from where he was sitting on the sand. "Be right back."

As soon as he's out of earshot, Simone says, "I knew I invited him for a reason."

I try to smile. "It's probably nice having him home. I bet you missed him."

"I did." She lies on her towel, and I do the same. We placed them close enough together to feel like we're on one giant towel instead of two separate ones. "I feel bad for him sometimes. All his friends are across the map. They all went to out-of-state colleges, so he doesn't have anyone to hang out with now."

"It was nice of you to invite him, then." I close my eyes, enjoying the way the sun heats my skin and turns the backs of my eyelids red. The smell of sunscreen in my nostrils is pungent. I could fall asleep right now.

"Two waters, as requested."

I open my eyes and see Nicolai handing Simone a bottle. He gives the second one to me, and I sip it gratefully. "Thanks, Nicolai."

"*Nicolai?*" Simone's voice is laced with humor and a giant laugh bursts from her lips. "Why did you call him that?" She sits up to look at me.

Shit. I forgot no one else calls him by his full name. "Um …" I look to Nicolai frantically for help.

"She heard Grandpa call me that at the party and thought it was cool," he says. "I told her it was my full name."

She narrows her eyes. "Where the hell was I?"

"Helping your mom with the food," I say, remembering she'd done that after introducing us.

"Oh." Simone lies back down. "Speaking of Mom, I think something's up with her."

"Like what?" Nicolai sits by our feet, propping himself up with one arm. He doesn't look at me, but I notice the tension in his shoulders. He's probably worried about Simone learning the extent of how bad things are with their parents.

"I don't know," she says, "but her and Dad have barely spoken to each other lately. It's weird. They're hiding something, I know it."

"Maybe you should ask them," I say, earning a glance from Nicolai. He doesn't look happy, but I don't care. Simone deserves to know what's going on, whether he likes it or not.

I try not to wince at the irony of that thought.

"It's not like they'd tell me the truth," she mutters. "I found a bunch of her things packed up, you know."

Nicolai casts his eyes downward. "Really? That's weird." Slowly, he glances up. "We'll have to ask her about it." There's so much weight in his statement, even though I know Simone is oblivious to it. I hear it though, in his inflection: it's finally time for her to know the truth about their parents.

Simone sighs. "I already asked her about it, and she said she was packing up some stuff to donate. But I've seen her using the stuff in the bags, more than once. God, I hate secrets. If there's one thing I can't stand, it's being lied to."

There's a beat of silence. The tension in the air between the three of us is unmistakable, so I stand up. "You know what? We should swim." I tug on Simone's hand, pulling her to her feet. "Come on. It will be fun!"

Her gaze jumps between the sea and my face. And then a grin stretches her lips. "Yeah. Okay, let's do it!" She motions Nicolai forward. "You coming?"

"Hell yeah, I'm coming!" A second later, he's racing ahead of us, toward the crashing water with me and Simone laughing at his heels.

Nicolai splashes straight into the icy water, fully submerging himself. When he comes back up, he shakes his hair out, reminding me of a dog after a bath. I cover my mouth to smother a laugh.

Simone tugs me back before I can jump in after him. "Wait! Can you swim while you're pregnant?" The words are whispered for only me to hear, and her eyes are round with concern.

But I wave away her hesitation. "Yes, it's fine!" I yank on her hand, taking her with me as I race forward. I cringe at how cold the water is, but once we're deep enough to either stand or tread water, my skin adjusts to the temperature.

Though it feels like only a few minutes, the three of us spend nearly an hour swimming, splashing, laughing. Nicolai pretends to be a shark and pulls on my ankle, and then Simone's, tugging each of us under briefly despite our comic, frantic screams. Simone dons her sunglasses, sliding them down from where they're perched atop her head, and shows us how to float on our backs by holding our breaths. I kick through the water and squeeze my toes around the sand, enjoying the squishy, wet, clay-like feeling.

By the time we make our way back to our towels, I'm exhausted. My body feels like a sponge, soaked and heavy with water, and I hug my arms around my waist to shield myself from the sting of the wind. My thighs start to burn as we traverse the sand to where our towels lie. Simone falls dramatically onto hers, and I'm about to continue forward and do the same, but something sharp cuts into my foot. I cry out. The sting of gritty sand in the open wound makes me wince and hop on one foot.

Nicolai pauses drying off to cast a concerned look in my direction.

"You okay?" Simone sits up and pulls her sunglasses back.

I reach down and touch my foot. It's gushing blood and there's a green shard of glass sticking out of it. "Mother fucker."

"Hold still," says Nicolai, dropping his towel. He holds my elbow so I can balance on one foot.

"I'm fine," I insist.

"I have a first aid kit in the car," says Simone. "I'll go get it." She runs off in the direction of the parking lot.

"Do you think you can make it back to where we were sitting?" Nicolai asks.

"Oh, yeah. Definitely." I limp, and then hop.

"Ev." Nicolai reaches for me. "Please, just let me help you."

"I got it."

The sound he makes sounds like a sigh and a laugh. "You look ridiculous."

"Shut up." I hop one more step but lose my balance and almost tumble onto the sand.

"Is it even safe to hop like that in your condition?"

I stop. "Actually, I'm not sure."

"Come here." He picks me up effortlessly, holding me with one arm under my legs and the other under my arms.

Our faces are inches apart and when I look at him, I momentarily get lost in his eyes. They look like portals that lead straight to the ocean behind us. "Thanks," I whisper. His arms as strong as pillars holding me up, and in them, I feel the steady beating of his heart.

When he sets me down on the towel, I squint into the distance and see Simone coming back. There's a white box in her hand.

Nicolai inspects my foot, gently removing the glass and brushing the sand away. I try not to jerk away against the pain and discomfort. Instead, I focus on his fingers, tickling the base of my foot. I feel every single touch travel up my leg and spread through my entire body.

"All right." Simone approaches us, opening the first aid kit and taking out several packages. "We got alcohol wipes, bandages, and some ointment."

She hands them to Nicolai, and he unwraps one of the paper squares. He works gently, dabbing at my injured foot with care. The air between us is charged with tension, and I try not to look at him as he works, afraid

I'll somehow reveal our secret attraction toward one another by doing so.

"Thanks," I tell Simone.

"No biggie. I'm glad I had a kit. Hopefully your foot will be okay."

"I'm sure it will."

Nicolai finishes bandaging me, and I flex my toes to make sure the bandage doesn't budge. It passes the test.

"My hero."

He grins. His face looks a little flushed. "Be careful." He pats my foot.

"No promises." I glance at the time on my phone. "We should probably start heading back if I'm going to be on time for school tonight."

"Yeah, of course. Let's get going."

We all make our way back to the car. I try not to put too much pressure on the base of my foot, using the front of my toes to keep my balance. When we're all buckled in and driving back, I get a text.

Nicolai: *Hang out again tomorrow?*

I hold my breath. It's not like Simone knows he just texted me, but it still feels obvious. I chance a look at him through the rearview mirror. His eyes meet mine.

Me: *We shouldn't.*

Nicolai: *Next week?*

Me: *Today wasn't good enough?*

Nicolai: *Not even close.*

Me: *Didn't you hear what your sister said? She can't take any more lies.*

Nicolai: *Let's tell her then.*

Me: *Tell her what exactly?*

It takes a moment for him to respond: *I don't know.*

I don't text him back.

I hug Simone when she stops in the street next to my car. "Thanks for today," I say. "I had fun."

"Sliced foot and all?" She half-smiles.

"Absolutely."

I glance into the backseat and give Nicolai an awkward salute. "See ya around."

"Most definitely."

I ignore that response, getting in my car and driving off. One more text from him comes through. I read it at the next red light.

You're due for a good hand, remember? Why not take a chance?

THIRTEEN

"You actually came," Nicolai says. He's waiting at the top of Communication Hill's long set of outdoor steps.

I stare up at him from the bottom, trying not to smile. "You asked nicely."

I almost decided not to come when he texted me earlier today. I imagined the way he'd look at me, sending desire through me with every glance. How pleased he'd be if I actually showed up. How much I'd regret seeing him afterward, back in my room with no other thoughts in my head but of him. It's been that way since the beach last week. I haven't been able to shake the way he held me after I cut my foot, both of us still wet from swimming, the heat of him warming me everywhere. Simone, stating how much she hates being lied to. And texting her after I got home to see if she finally learned the truth about her mom, but not getting a response.

And yet, here I am.

The day is bright and warm. The steps are mostly

empty, save for me and Nicolai, and the occasional joggers weaving around me as I walk up the long flight of steps. He's wearing gray sweatpants and a black shirt that stretches tightly across his chest and arms. His hair is tied up in a bun, showing off his defined jaw. Something catches my eye next to him, and I belatedly notice he's brought a dog along.

"Who's this?" I hold my hand out for the dog to sniff, because that's what I always see other people doing around dogs. I've never spent much time around them, since Mariah is terribly allergic.

"This is Rolf." He smiles fondly at the enormous canine. "I rescued him a few years ago from the pound. He was next on their kill list."

"Why?"

"Pit bulls typically don't last long in shelters. You know, with the stigma that they're dangerous and all," he says. "I had to hide him in my dorm when I lived on campus, but he's well behaved, so no one but my roommates ever knew."

"Has he been at your house all this time? I never noticed him before."

"He's kind of a lazy boy. Spends a lot of time sleeping at the foot of my parents' bed. I told him today he needed to get out and exercise with me. No more loafing around."

I squat next to Rolf to get a better look at him. His fur is short and dark brown, and there's a mask of white surrounding his eyes. He licks me, and I fall back in astonishment.

Nicolai laughs. "I think he likes you."

"Is that so?" I wipe slobber off my cheek.

He pats the dog's head. "You'll have to get in line, my friend."

I press my lips together to keep from smiling. Somehow, the fact that he has a dog—especially one he rescued—makes him even more attractive.

I inhale sharply through my nose. "Why did you invite me here, Nicolai? We just saw each other last week."

We're walking along a trail hugging a set of large houses. The view down at the street-level neighborhoods is breathtaking, and I bask in the feeling of the warm breeze in my hair.

"What do you mean?" His eyes round in feigned innocence. "We're friends. Can't friends see each other more than once a week?"

I arch an eyebrow at him. "Did you tell Simone you'd be here with me?"

His smile fades. "No."

"Exactly,'" I say. "I don't see why we should have to keep our *friendship* a secret if that's all it is."

We walk together in silence along the trail. I glance at the joggers who pass us, wondering what it must be like for people who do this regularly. How nice it must be to have time to jog in a pretty neighborhood.

"There's another reason I asked you to come here with me," he finally says.

"Oh?"

"I've been meaning to tell you I did some digging on your dad, Leland Jones. I hope that's okay," he adds, catching a glance of my surprised expression. "Because I found something weird."

A bubble of unwarranted hope makes my knees wobble. "What do you mean? What did you find?"

"When I searched your dad's name, a Facebook profile came up." He clasps the back of his neck. "But the person's name was Leland Doorsy and then, in parentheses, Leland Jones. Like he might have changed his name from one to the other at some point. Who knows?"

"Okay." I shrug. "So some guy has the same name. That's not too weird."

"I messaged him," says Nicolai. "And asked him if he knows your mom, Mariah Martin. He said they went to high school together. They used to date."

I stop walking, suddenly feeling like I might pass out. My head spins, so I tilt it down and grip my knees.

"Are you okay?" He reaches out to steady me.

"My parents never went to high school together," I tell him, head still down. "My mom said that she met my dad at a party. They had a one-night stand and then he died."

Silence. And then, "I'm sorry, Ev. I was only trying to help. I probably shouldn't have—"

"No." I straighten, my vision clearing. "It's not you who should be apologizing. But I don't understand why my mom would lie. There has to be some mistake."

"I'm sure there is." He tries to sound reassuring. "You should ask her if she even knows him. Maybe he was trolling and happens to share the same name as your dad."

"I doubt that," I mutter. "I'm not saying a damn thing

to my mom. I don't want her to keep me from learning the truth. I'm going to message Leland before I bring it up."

He watches me warily. "I'll send you his profile. Hang on." He takes out his phone, and I do the same. An alert appears on my screen.

Nicolai Beckett sent you a friend request.

I accept it and then put my phone away. As eager as I am to see what Leland looks like, I want to do it in private. I have a feeling I might cry, and I don't want to do it in front of Nicolai. "Thanks for sending me his page. I can't wait to tell Simone about this."

We continue on, and my mind is a whirl of new possibilities. Could it be possible that Leland is my dad, that my mom didn't know he was still alive? Maybe she received false information. Maybe all this time, he's been trying to find her, too.

There's so much I need to process.

"Simone is kind of going through a hard time right now," he says, breaking the silence and bringing me back to the present.

I frown. "What happened?" But there's only one thing he can mean. Only one secret bigger than the two of us sneaking around together. My blood runs cold. "No," I say. "She knows?"

He looks solemn. "She's known since the beach."

"How did she find out?"

"She demanded to know the truth when we got home. She forced my parents to tell her everything."

"You didn't prepare her first?" I smack his arm. "What the hell, Nico?"

"Woah," he says, holding up his hands in surrender. "How is this my fault? I thought you wanted her to find out."

"You could have warned her first to lessen the blow! I bet she was caught completely off guard."

"Seriously? This is my fault now?" He looks thrown, like he can't believe I'm mad at him, but also like he kind of wants to laugh.

"No. I guess not." I sigh deeply. "How is she handling it? Was it ugly?"

"Oh, it was ugly," he says darkly. "Once the can of worms was opened, my parents started yelling at each other."

"And Simone?"

He cringes. "There were tears involved. Let's leave it at that."

I frown. "I wonder why she didn't answer my text."

"I believe her exact words were, 'I don't want to talk to anyone ever again.'" He cringes.

"I'm going to call her later."

He smiles faintly. "I'm sure she'd like that."

We get to the end of the trail and stop so Rolf can drink from a bowl under the water fountain. Jesus. This place even caters to dogs.

I glance at Nicolai, sweating from our walk. The sun illuminates his skin in a healthy glow, accentuating the freckles on his nose, like the soft, warm sand from the beach. He leans over and rubs his dog's head, a tender look in his aquatic eyes. Something tugs in my chest at the sight.

When Rolf is done drinking, Nicolai looks up. "Ready?"

"Yep," I say. "Let's keep going."

I can feel his stare on me as we finish our walk, but I try to ignore it. If I let myself get wrapped up in the heat from his gaze, I might do something I'll regret.

"That's a pretty house," I say, pointing down the hill to an isolated townhouse with a fenced yard. But it's just one of many, so I add, "They're all pretty."

"They are," he agrees, and then after a long pause, asks, "If you could live anywhere in the world, money aside, where would it be?"

Anywhere in the world? I've never really thought about it. Not because I don't care, but because my options have always been so slim. But there is one place I've always wanted to go. "Probably New York."

He tilts his head. "How come?"

"There are so many people there. I'd never be alone." My voice takes on a dream-like tone as I stare down at the houses below us, sprinkled throughout the grassy expanse of hills and surrounding us like daisies in a field. When I snap out of my reverie, my gaze jumps to Nicolai. He's watching me, fascinated, eyes narrowed and lips slightly parted. "What?"

He hides a grin and shrugs. "Nothing. It's just that a wise girl once told me it's nice to be alone because people are the cause of everything bad."

My mind flashes back to our first date. I can't help but be a little surprised that he remembers.

Nicolai's phone rings, so I fall back to give him

privacy while he answers. "Mom?" His shoulders seem to tense as he talks. After a few minutes, he hangs up.

"Time to go?" I ask.

He puts his phone away and smirks. "Why? Trying to get rid of me?"

"Maybe," I say. But really, I'm hoping for the opposite.

He laughs. "We're at the end of the trail anyway. There's the parking lot." He points ahead of us.

"Oh." My excitement fades away as we walk down the final steps leading to where our cars are parked. Neither of us get in. I rest my hand on the handle of my car, but don't move. I don't want to leave yet, and I'm annoyed with myself because of it. In fact, I probably shouldn't have even come here today. Every minute I spend with him only strengthens my attraction for him. It only complicates things.

"Bye, Ev." He turns around and opens the door to get in his car.

My heart clenches. "Wait." Slowly he turns back around, and I take a step toward him, opening my arms. Wordlessly, he pulls me against him.

It starts out as a hug. Really. But my hands seem to have a mind of their own as they slide up his chest and touch his face. And then he looks at me. He slides his arms down, around my waist, bringing me even closer.

We haven't crossed a line yet. This could be considered a friendly embrace. And though every muscle in me is desperate for Nicolai to cross that invisible line, he doesn't. He lets me go and backs away.

It's not what I want. But it's what I need.

"Bye." Still, I can't stop myself from brushing a fleeting kiss on his cheek. A friendly kiss, really. And then I get in my car, ignoring the way his eyes seem to strain as they watch me.

I want to smack myself. Being friends with him is pointless. He knows I'm attracted to him, and I can tell he feels the same way about me. And Simone isn't the biggest obstacle standing between us. I know there's a chance she would be okay with her best friend and her brother being together. Maybe not right now, while she already has enough going on, but later she might be.

My growing feelings for Nicolai feel wrong because I'm pregnant with another man's child. And if that man is John, I know deep down I'll want to work things out with him. If that happens, what's beginning to blossom between me and Nicolai will only make it harder to follow through.

The worst part is what I feel is more than just attraction. He's someone I can be honest with. Someone I can talk to. And I haven't had that in a really, *really* long time.

He does the most dangerous thing a person can do; he lets me hope.

And this kind of hope—the kind that makes me feel like somehow everything's going to turn out okay in the end—will only end in disappointment.

The house is dark when I get home. I flip on the light switch, but nothing happens. The electricity must be out.

"Fucking wonderful," I say aloud. In a few hours it will be time to pick up Amma from school and drop her off at Jaycee's for a playdate. But I won't be able to hide this from her when she comes home.

I plop down on the couch and cover my face with both hands. The weight of everything I'm going through is becoming too much for me.

Numbly, I walk to my room, digging down through my underwear drawer until I touch my notebook.

I bring it back to the couch, using my phone as a light, and write:

your presence is like a prescription for my denial
& that you love me,
despite who I am & what I've done,
is the diagnosis I refuse to accept.

I'm not sure who the poem is about. My mom? God? Nicolai? Anyone and everyone? The thought is so depressing.

I decide to text Simone: *Have you talked to your mom yet?*

And she responds within a few minutes: *Haven't had a chance yet!*

I frown. Seriously? She's going to lie? But, why? Does she not feel confident enough in our friendship to tell me, even though I confided in her about my pregnancy?

I shake my head slowly. I can't afford to sit here feeling sorry for myself. I have to figure out what Mariah is hiding.

I open Facebook on my phone and scroll through my

messages until I find the link Nicolai sent me to Leland Jones's profile.

I click on his picture.

He's a friendly-looking dark-skinned man with brown hair. It's not red. This disappoints me. I always thought I got my red hair from my dad, like a parting gift from him before he died. At least, that's who Mariah said I got it from.

But this man may not be my father.

I send him a message with shaky, trembling hands. *Hi. My name is Everly. I'm Mariah Martin's daughter. This might seem random, but I have some questions for you, if that's all right. Would you be willing to meet?*

I regret sending the message the instant after it happens. What if Mariah lied about my dad being dead for a good reason? Maybe Leland is dangerous. But why wouldn't she tell me if that were the case?

I need to know the truth. And speaking of the truth, I need to tell John about the paternity testing, but in a way that doesn't seem like I'm asking him to pay for it. Just mention it, offhand. That way, if he *wants* to pay for it, he can make the decision himself, without feeling like I'm pressuring him into shelling out a couple grand.

As soon as I find out the results, I can finally view my circumstances with a clear head. I feel like I'm straddling a state line, with each foot in a different state.

Numbly, I dial John's number.

FOURTEEN

"Everly?" John's voice is pleasant, curious.

"Hey, John," I say into the phone. I don't know why I'm so nervous. I should just ask him if he's willing to pay for the testing and be done with it. But the words don't leave my mouth. Asking people for things, especially *money*, is like offering up my right arm to a stranger. Impossible.

"I've been meaning to call you, actually." His voice cuts into my internal struggle. "I was hoping you'd let me buy you some maternity supplies."

I frown. "What do you mean?"

"Well, there are things you'll need in order to have a smooth, healthy pregnancy. And I'd like to be the one to buy them for you." A pause. "Is that all right?"

"Uh ..." I laugh shakily, "sure. I guess."

"Great." His voice has an upbeat lilt to it. "Can you meet me at the department store in downtown San Jose, or do you need me to drive you?"

I lower my phone from my ear to check the time. Amma will need to be home from Jaycee's house by dinnertime. Even though Jaycee's mom told me her daughter had been excited to play with Amma, and that Amma could stay as late as she wanted, I don't feel comfortable letting Jaycee's mother feed her.

"I have some time. I can meet you there," I tell John. "But I'll need to be back in a few hours because I have school tonight."

"Not a problem," he assures me. "I'll meet you there."

He hangs up, and I'm left wondering how my attempt to ask him to pay for DNA testing turned into him buying me pregnancy stuff.

Because you have no backbone. It's all I come up with as I gather my shit to meet him.

The department store downtown is bustling. Cars weave in and out of the parking lot, swiping empty parking spots as soon as they appear. The sun will be going down soon, and the sidewalks are crammed with people.

When I enter the store, I send John a text. *I'm here.*

His response comes through. *Me too. Near the front.*

I squint through the fluorescent lighting of the entrance until I catch sight of him waiting by the coffee stand. When he sees me, he waves a long-fingered hand in the air.

I make my way over. He's dressed in slacks and a blue button-up, much like the one he wore the day we met at the bar. It makes his white skin look healthy and his muted blue eyes slightly more prominent.

He nods at me. "Everly."

"John," I say, mocking his polite tone.

But he doesn't catch it. He picks up a shopping basket from the stand next to us and we walk toward the medicine aisle of the store. "You should be taking prenatal vitamins," he says.

As soon as we're in front of all the different bottles, he scans them with a focused expression. He picks one up, reading the back, and puts it back.

I shift my weight from one foot to the other. "Aren't they all the same?"

"No." He picks up another, reading the back until he's satisfied. "This one is good, though."

"I forget you're a doctor sometimes."

He smiles warmly. "I've been meaning to ask you if you're willing to consider circumcision if the baby is a male."

His question takes me aback. "John, we don't even know if you're the father yet. Why are you asking me that?"

"It's important to be on the same page with things like that." He presses his lips into a line.

I sigh deeply. "Well, sorry. I haven't even thought about it." He's acting like I'm going to give birth tomorrow, and it's stressing me out. "I'd rather take all this one step at a time if you don't mind."

"Fine." His lips turn down.

"I think the first step is finding out if you're the father, don't you?"

"Yes. Of course."

We continue walking, this time toward the clothing aisle.

"What are we getting now?"

He frowns. "You're going to need maternity clothes, aren't you?"

"Yes, but ..." I stop in place. "John, I think it's really nice that you want to get me all this stuff. But it doesn't feel right. Not until I know if the baby is yours or not."

"Okay." He stops walking too. "I assume you have an OBGYN by now. You should make an appointment and have the first ultrasound done. I'd really like to be there."

My spine tingles with guilt. "Actually, I already did that."

Pain flickers in his eyes. "Oh."

"I'm sorry. I didn't realize you'd want to come. It's so early."

He sighs. "I would have loved to. But that's fine. I'll come to the next one. And we can ask to have non-invasive testing done, if you're willing. I'd be more than happy to pay for it. It can be quite pricey."

The weight in my bones seems to lift. "I would love that." I cover my hand with his, and he meets my gaze. "Thank you."

He smiles faintly. "Can I at least buy you the prenatal?"

I laugh. "Sure. But that's it."

We make our way to the register. Out of the corner of my eye, I see a pregnant woman who must be in her final trimester, because her belly protrudes from her body at a painful-looking distance. I try not to cringe. Being here with John, shopping and hearing him talk about the baby as if it's already here, it's too much for me.

It doesn't make sense. His support and his eagerness to be a parent with me is exactly what I should want in a prospective baby daddy. I should be happy he wants to be so involved. But it doesn't feel right. Probably because it's too good to be true. With my luck, Vaughn is the father of this child. But even if he's not, why is my gut instinct to push all this away? Because of Nicolai?

John buys the bottle of prenatal vitamins and hands it to me, a resigned smile on his face. I try to smile back. I thank him. And I hope with all my heart that Nicolai has nothing to do with my sudden reluctance.

When I stop the car in front of Jaycee's house, Amma is already waiting outside. *Good girl,* I think. I've trained her well. I've nailed it into her that when I give her a time to meet me outside, I mean that time. She knows I have class tonight, so she didn't try to barter and squeeze more time out of her playdate when I dropped her off.

"Did you have fun?" I ask when she gets in the car. Her face is covered in stage makeup—blue eyeshadow, red lipstick, and fake eyelashes. "Oh, my God, Amma." I smother my laugh with my hand.

"Jaycee sucks at makeup," she tells me flatly. "I did a much better job on her. It's not fair."

She tells me about her day as I drive across town to get Mariah from work. When she holds up a drawing she did of Thor, I take one look at that long blond hair and immediately think of Nicolai.

Blushing, I change the subject. "You finished your homework, right?"

Her shoulders droop. "Yes, sis."

"Good."

When we get to Mariah's work, she's waiting at her usual spot on the curb. She perks up when I flash the headlights in her face.

"Hi, mija," she says, getting in eagerly. She twists in her seat after buckling to ruffle Amma's hair. "Hi, sweetheart. Wow. Look at your beautiful makeup."

Amma offers her a bland expression. "It's not beautiful, Mom. Jaycee is clearly not an artist."

Mariah laughs so hard her dimples show. "Your words, not mine," she wheezes.

"How was work, Mom?" I ask. We're almost home, so this is the only chance I'll have to talk to her until tomorrow, since I have class tonight.

She reaches over and rubs my arm. "Just fine. I got some good tips tonight. Listened to music on my break. Someone sent back an untouched plate of meatloaf, and Kirk let me eat it for lunch."

We talk about the small details of her day the rest of the drive. I love hearing them, because it makes me feel like a fly on the wall, like I got to spend the day with her even though it's the opposite of true.

And it never lasts long enough for me. Amma and Mariah get out of the car, and then I drive to school. Night classes used to be my favorite. I used to love driving in the dark with hardly anyone else on the road to slow me down. But now, I can barely stay awake.

I park in the upper level of the parking garage and sling my backpack over my shoulder. I take the elevator down to ground level and walk through the vacant corridor to my engineering class. The flickering light bathes the hallway with an ominous vibe, but as soon as I step into the classroom, I'm surrounded by students in their seats. The instructor, Mr. Samuels, is at the front, reading over his plan for today's lesson. People are still talking to one another since class hasn't started yet. I sit in the front row next to a girl who's reviewing her notes from last class.

A wave of exhaustion suddenly hits me. I bury my head in my arms. And when class starts, I struggle to sit up straight and keep my eyes open.

Mr. Samuels begins his lecture, but I'm not paying attention. Not only am I too tired, but seeing John earlier is at the front of my mind. After today, my pregnancy no longer feels like a future problem that I have plenty of time to sort out. Now, it feels impending, like my life ending is on a timer. And I don't have enough time.

I peer over my shoulder at my classmates. Faces forward. Bright eyes, hungry for learning. Gazes alight with interest. Fingers typing on laptops and writing with pens.

But not me. I hate this class. I hate engineering, but it's my ticket to a better life. Getting my degree is going to help me get out of the hellhole of a situation I'm in.

So I straighten my spine. I rub the sleep from my eyes. And I try my best to pay attention.

FIFTEEN

"She was cute," says Simone.

I arch an eyebrow. "Who?"

"The client who just left." Simone points at the entrance of The Arbor Salon with her chin.

I just got to work to close the salon with Vaughn, and Simone's shift is about to end. It feels like it's been forever since I was scheduled with her and seeing her here makes me miss it even more. Besides, she still hasn't talked to me about her parents, despite my subtle hints and questions regarding the matter.

I type on the computer. "You mean Elle Henderson of Lincoln Avenue?" I point at the client information section of the screen. "Here's her phone number if you want to call her."

She looks horrified. "Um, yeah, if I want to look like a total stalker!" She gently smacks my arm. "What the hell, Everly?"

"Saves time this way."

Simone laughs, and I disguise mine as a cough when Willow walks over to the front desk. "Simone, you can go ahead and clock out. The last client just left."

I move out of the way. Simone clocks out and picks up her stuff from the small shelf behind us. "See you later, Ever," she says.

I wave. "Bye."

After Willow leaves, Vaughn and I begin our closing routine.

I sweep a pile of dark hair from under a stylist's station. I'm glad he and I are working tonight because I'm planning on telling him I scheduled paternity testing for the baby. He'll probably be grateful to know this mess will be over sooner rather than later.

"Hey, Everly," he says from the stockroom. "Come here."

The hairs on my arm stand up, but I sweep the hair into the dustpan, dump it in the garbage, and head to where he's waiting. *You are in control here, Everly,* I remind myself. *Not him.*

I peek through the doorway of the stockroom, where Vaughn is waiting next to his clothes, which are in a pile on the floor. Panic forms in my throat, but I swallow it down. "No thanks," I say as cheerfully as I can. "You have nothing on me now, Vaughn. Our arrangement ended a long time ago."

"Not so fast," he says, like we have all the time in the world. "There's no reason to stop anything. It's not like you can get *double* pregnant. I know you have a thing for that guy who hit me, but he doesn't have to know what happens between us. I won't tell."

He can't be serious. If I weren't so afraid, I might laugh at his idiocy. "Vaughn, there is nothing, *nothing* between us. There never was. You're completely delusional if you think otherwise." I turn on my heel, ready to book it for the exit, but he grabs my wrist and pulls me into the tiny room with him. He shuts the door and locks it behind him.

"Open the door," I demand.

"Not until we talk about this."

"Talk about what?" I sound scared, no matter how hard I'm trying to hide it, and it pisses me off.

"You said there's nothing between us, but I beg to differ."

"If you're talking about the baby, I already scheduled an appointment to find out which of you is the father," I say. "I really hope it's John so I can be rid of you once and for all. Now let me out."

He narrows his eyes. "I'm not talking about that *thing*, I'm talking about us!" He gets louder, sending a fresh wave of terror through me, but I refuse to show it. *Straighten your spine, Everly, and show him you're not weak.*

"There is no *us*. It's over, Vaughn. Even if the baby is yours, I want nothing to do with you." My voice breaks at the end. I stifle a sob. The last thing I want to do is get emotional, but dammit, if the baby is his, my heart might actually break.

"Forget the testing," he mutters. "I told you to get rid of it."

I take a step toward him and shove him hard on the chest. "It's not up to you!"

He stares me down. A momentous rage seems to build

up inside him, and he says, "You know, it really hurt my feelings, what you said that day in your room a while ago."

"What are you talking about?" I clench my hands into fists to hide the fact that my fingers are trembling.

"You said I was just a dumbass with no cards left to play." He lets the words hang in the air between us before grabbing my wrists and turning me around. I try to scream, but he pins my hands to the wall with one of his and covers my mouth with the other. "How about now, Everly? How about now? Who's the dumbass this time? Let's see *you* play a card."

I thrash as hard as I can, kicking and squirming until I'm out of his grip. I reach for the nearest hard object in the room. I don't even look at what it is before I smash it over his head with all my strength.

"What the fuck?" he yells. Broken glass falls down his face, onto the floor, everywhere. His face is bleeding. It looks like the object I grabbed was a mirror.

"If you ever put your hands on me again, I will turn you in for everything. The blackmail, the groping. Everything. You'll become a registered sex offender. Now, fuck off!" I run past him, fumble with the lock and stumble out of the stockroom—out of the salon, and into the parking lot, which is mostly empty now that it's dark out. I have no idea if he's going to try to follow me, but at least I have a head start, considering he'll need to get dressed before he can go anywhere.

"Keys," I mutter, searching the empty air around me. "I forgot my keys in the salon." Tears sting my eyes. There's no way in hell I'm going back in there. I may have threatened him, but I don't want to wait around and see if he'll try hurting me again. I have more than myself to think about. There's the baby, too. I pat my back pocket and when I touch my phone, I almost cry in relief. At least I didn't forget that, too.

I duck behind a massive topiary bush and call the first person I can think of. He answers on the first ring. "Nicolai?"

"Everly?"

"I need you to come pick me up. Please."

He sounds worried. "Where the hell are you?"

"I'm at work."

"I'll be right there." And then he hangs up.

While I wait, I try to control the involuntary trembling of my body. I remind myself that Vaughn got what he deserved back there. I protected myself. I stood up to him, all on my own.

And now I'm hiding behind a giant plant.

Standing here, in the still night with no one else around, the thundering of my heart sounds too loud. With shaky thumbs, I type into my notes:

Bricks
by Everly Jean Martin

i am a house
and you tear me down
brick by brick
cracking my walls as you
p l u c k
each piece

from my foundation
to build a house of your own.
well, i tell you
as you take my bricks
tear down my house
and build yourself up
keep them, they're cracked
keep each piece of me you take.
i say, nice try
but you cannot take & thrive on
cannot ever survive on
what's already
b r o k e n

The tires of Nicolai's car screech as they approach me several minutes later. I step out from behind my bush and wave my arms in the air before he can pass me.

He stops and I reach for the handle, but he gets out of the car. "What happened?" He takes my face in his hands, his eyes searching. "Why were you *hiding*? What's going on?"

My lips part. I don't know why I'm afraid to tell him. I swallow the lump in my throat and shift my gaze to the salon.

He follows the direction I'm looking and clenches his jaw. "It's Vaughn, isn't it?"

I nod. Tug on the sleeve of his jacket. "Let's just go."

"Did he hurt you?"

"He pinned me against the wall," I whisper. "He covered my mouth, and he *scared* me, but that's it. I smashed him over the head with a mirror after that and ran." I let out a single sad, and pathetic chuckle.

But Nicolai doesn't so much as blink. His eyes are hard. "Where is he?"

"In the stockroom. I left my keys in there."

He opens the passenger side door. The engine is still running, and puffs of smoky exhaust pool around our ankles as I get in. The heater is on, and I bring my hands closer to the vent, letting it warm me to my bones.

"Stay here," says Nicolai. "Lock the doors. I'll be right back."

I tense. "What are you going to do?"

"I'm going to teach him to keep his hands to himself. Be right back."

Before I can utter another word, he's rushing into the salon. I exhale slowly and lock the doors. Sinking into the seat of the car, I close my eyes, suddenly feeling terribly exhausted.

When he comes back, I unlock the door and he gets in. "Here are your keys." He hands them to me, and I curl my fingers around them, letting the metal dig into my skin. "Are you going to be all right?"

"I'll be okay. Thanks, Nico." I touch his face. My fingertips meet a fine layer of stubble.

He leans in, his eyes closing against my touch. And I can't help it. I close the distance between us and kiss him on the cheek. The proximity draws me in.

I want so much more than this, and I want it with him. The realization hits me hard and fast; unexpected and overwhelming.

It terrifies me.

"Do you still need a ride?" he asks, opening his eyes.

"No. I have my keys now, thanks to you." I hold them up and jingle them between us. "You didn't murder Vaughn, did you? Because I need him to show up for DNA testing next week."

"I promise he'll survive."

"Thank you." I smile faintly. "Good night, Nicolai." I get out of his car and into mine. He waits for me to drive off before he leaves the parking lot.

SIXTEEN

When I get home, the first thing I do is grab my notebook. I can hear the combined snoring of Mariah and Amma coming from their bedroom, but there's no way I can sleep right now.

After everything that happened, I'm feeling tired, sad, scared, and very uneasy. The shock of tonight is just now registering.

Dear Everly,

You can't describe what it's like to have only yourself to talk to. Your tormented thoughts, staining this paper, the ink invading the blank page like a disease.

Your thoughts do the same to your soul.

They won't go away. They pierce any hope, any small glimmer or bubble, like a needle through a fine layer of skin.

You wonder if skin can grow an outer shell. A protective layer. You wonder if hope has any protection of its own. If it does, you need it to find you because it's getting lonely here, and you could really use a friend. It feels like if you crumble, so will everyone else around you. Mariah and Amma don't realize how much you're carrying, and just how close you are to breaking.

> *be happy, they say*
> *be happy*
> *but not you, Everly.*
> *you don't force your own cheeks to carry*
> *the heavy burden of a*
> *fake smile*
> *be sad, you say*
> *be sad*
> *for the heart cannot know true happiness*
> *until it first experiences*
> *true pain*

I toss the notebook angrily back into my underwear drawer. Before I can think things through, I'm driving to John's house. I doubt Mariah will notice me leaving, considering it's still the middle of the night and she's out like a light. Since finding out about Leland, I've been avoiding her. I know she's noticed, but she hasn't said anything. So if she wakes up and finds me gone, I doubt she'll confront me.

Thinking of Vaughn brings tears to my eyes. I drive faster.

All the lights are off at John's when I park in the mile-long driveway, but thankfully his car is here.

I hesitate before I knock on the door. It's the middle of the night. He might be sleeping. And even if he's not, what reason do I have to barge in on him like this right now?

The porch light turns on and the door opens. His brown hair is mussed from sleeping. "Everly?" He squints at me against the bright light. "What are you doing here? Is everything okay?" He's wearing black silk pajamas with the initials *JT* embossed on them.

"JT?" I ask, pointing to the pocket on his shirt.

"Johnathan Taylor."

"Oh. Got it." I probably look like a maniac, coming here in the middle of the night like this, hair in tangled knots and makeup smeared from crying earlier.

John looks concerned. "Do you want to come inside?" He places a hand on my back and leads me in, and I sit on the sofa. "Here. You look cold." He hands me a giant, fluffy blanket. I wrap it around my shoulders. It's a thick material, soft and heavy. The weight of it cocoons me.

He brings me a hot mug, and I take a sip. It's tea. After everything I've been through tonight, it makes me smile. It's perfect, warming my insides despite the coldness in my heart. Tea is so ... John.

He sits in the chair across from me. We're separated by the coffee table, and an ornate grandfather clock ticks on the wall behind him. "Is something wrong?" He winces when he looks at my stomach. "Is the baby ...?"

"No!" I realize in an instant what he's thinking. "Nothing's wrong with the baby. Sorry, I should have said so sooner."

He visibly relaxes. "Good. What is it then?"

I take a deep breath. "I'm starting to have second thoughts about this whole thing." I close my eyes as soon as the sentence leaves my mouth. I can't bear to see the look on his face.

"You don't mean that." His voice wavers like a blanket in the wind.

"I do." It would be so much easier to ignore my feelings, but why did I come, if not to confide in him? "Vaughn is such a terrible person. What if he's the father? I know it's only a fifty-fifty chance, but even that's enough to make me want to end this."

He frowns. "Why are you telling me this now? Did something happen tonight?"

"He got aggressive with me at work tonight. He borderline attacked me. What else is new?"

John's nostrils flare. "That's completely unacceptable. I'm going to call the police." He stands up.

"Relax." I grab his arm, careful not to let the tea slosh over the sides of my cup. "I can handle Vaughn myself just fine. That's not why I'm telling you this."

A pool of red appears on John's white cheeks. "Then let me beat the shit out of him!"

His fury catches me off guard. I expected him to remain cool and collected as usual. "Just sit down." I take my previous seat and touch the spot next to me. John sighs and sits.

"I cannot call myself a man," he says through clenched teeth, "if I let this slide. It's wrong. How could you tell me this and expect me not to do anything?"

"Don't worry. If he ever touches me again, he'll wish he never met me. I don't need you to rescue me, John. I just need you to understand that he's the reason I don't want this."

"But I *do* want this," he says. He takes my hand, forcing me to look at those sad blue eyes of his. "I want this more than anything. Doesn't that matter?"

I cast my gaze downward. I can't stand the way my heart clenches as he tells me this.

"There's too much to consider," I say. "I haven't finished school. I don't have enough money to take care of a child. You and I barely know each other. We're not in a relationship. I can't do this alone—"

"You won't be alone," he insists. "I'll be here every step of the way. You're forgetting that when it's the key factor here."

I can't deny that his words comfort me. But he's wrong. Promising to help me, to be involved, is no longer the key factor in all this. It might have been when those two pink lines first appeared, but it's not anymore. What matters is my heart. And right now, it's torn between doing what's right for my baby and letting down its defenses for the person who—despite my efforts—has managed to wriggle his way in.

"John, I need you to be honest with me. Are you really as set on becoming a parent as you're making it seem? Because if not, now's the time to tell me. I'd be going through with this mainly for you. Ending the pregnancy would make my life a whole lot easier."

He nods, his head bobbing like a buoy on a lake. "I know. I really do. You have no idea how much this means to me, Everly. Thank you."

John returns to his seat. He lets his head fall back, like a huge weight has been lifted off his shoulders. Like in promising to let my world completely crumble, I've just single handedly patched his back together.

―――――――

I'd thought seeing John would help. I really did. But back in the comfort of my bed, staring at the ceiling, the burning in my throat is impossible to ignore. A few tears slide down the sides of my eyes, pooling in my hair on the pillow. I don't wipe them away. I don't try to think about something else to make it better. I just let myself cry silently.

It feels like this night will never end. And though I know all I have to do is sleep to skip time and bring tomorrow to me, I can't close my eyes without trembling with fear. I feel too vulnerable.

When I get a text message, my heart stutters. I know before I even check that it's Nicolai. *You up?*

I close my eyes, pressing the phone to my chest. Just knowing he cares makes me feel less alone. I respond, *No*, knowing it will make him smile.

Nicolai: *Funny. How are you feeling?*

Me: *I'm fine. Thanks for getting my keys.*

Nicolai: *Of course. Anytime.*

I stare at the words on the screen, and a sob builds in my throat. I know it's partly pregnancy hormones and shock. But I bite down on my pillow and let myself scream, muffling it as best I can. A few strangled sobs come out.

I don't want to be alone tonight.

I sniff, swiping at my eyes. And then I send another message to Nicolai. *Actually, I lied. I'm not fine.*

His response is instant. *What's wrong? Did something else happen?*

I type numbly. *Nothing is wrong. I just don't want to be alone.*

Nicolai: *Do you want me to come over?*

Me: *Normally I'd say no.* I swear mentally. I want him to come over more than anything. Why is that so hard for me to admit? Does it make me weak to want him, to need him tonight? I really hope not. I'm so tired of trying to be strong all the time. I think if I can allow myself one moment of weakness, that it will make being strong again that much easier.

Nicolai replies, *I'm going to take that as a yes.*

As friends of course, I write back. I don't want to give him the wrong idea. I'm not inviting him over for sex. It's the last thing on my mind.

But he types back, *Of course.* It makes my chest feel lighter.

He's coming. Nicolai is coming here, just to be with me. I exhale deeply, letting the tension in my body loosen.

I tiptoe out of bed and wait by the window to watch for his car. It takes about fifteen minutes for him to arrive, and when I see him taking the stairs two at a time, I open the door before he can knock.

And then we're face to face. Those thick brows narrow as his gaze searches my face tenderly.

I wrap my arms around his neck, letting the warmth radiating from him settle over my skin.

"Hey," I whisper.

"Hey," he says into my hair, his voice equally quiet.

I pull away from him. "Come on." I capture his hand in mine and take him through the living room. We take quiet, slow steps until we cross the hallway and step into my room. Nicolai has never been here before, but it's so dark, it doesn't feel like an official visit. Otherwise, I'd probably worry about what he thinks of my less-than-ideal surroundings.

I pull him into my room and shut the door. And then I can breathe again. "My mom would flip if she knew you were in here."

His outline is visible in front of me after a few blinks. "It's a good thing she'll never find out," he says quietly.

"I don't know why it matters. She would only be worried about you getting me pregnant." I huff out an uneven laugh. "No use stressing about that though." I walk across my room and sit on the edge of my bed. Nicolai comes closer and reaches out, taking my chin in his hand and rubbing my jaw with timid movements that seem to stretch out time and double the tension in the air between us.

I scoot back on the bed to make room for him until I hit the wall and pat the empty spot next to me. "There's plenty of room."

He hesitates. "Are you sure that's a good idea?"

I want to laugh. What was he expecting? To sit on the floor? It's not like we've never been in a bed together. But knowing him, he's probably just trying to be respectful, especially knowing Vaughn attacked me tonight. He's probably being cautious in case I don't want to be touched. But having him next to me is anything but threatening. It's the most comforting thing I can fathom. "Please." I peel back the blanket. "As friends. I just want to lie here with you. That's all."

The outline of his body relaxes. He lowers himself onto the bed, careful not to let the mattress creak.

I scoot closer and drape my arm over his chest, and he reciprocates, covering me with his other arm.

With my face pressed into the crook of his neck, I inhale the scent of his skin. It smells like fresh laundry mixed with aftershave. "You smell nice," I tell him.

"So do you." He traces shapes on my forearm with his index finger. "What were you doing before I got here?"

I tense. For some reason, I don't want to tell him that I went to see John. So I tell him what I was doing before that. "Writing."

"School stuff?"

I contemplate lying, saying yes. But I want to tell him the truth. I want him to know me, no matter how much the idea scares me. I swallow my unease. "No. I was writing in my journal."

"You have a journal?"

"I know it sounds silly," I say. "Immature, even."

"Not at all." He smooths my hair with his hand. "I think journals are cool. What do you write about?"

I try to ignore the fluttering in my heart as I answer him. "My shitty life, mostly. Some poems every now and then. It's better than talking about all my problems and being a burden."

He stills, then pulls his face away from mine to squint at me through the dark. "A burden? Is that what you think?"

I shrug. I can't look him in the eye, because, yes, it's exactly what I think, no matter how ridiculous he makes it sound.

"You're not a burden, Everly." He aligns our faces side by side on the pillow, so I'm forced to look at him. "You can talk to me, or anyone else, anytime."

I want to believe him so badly. And maybe someday I will. But for now, I think I'll stick to my journal. "Maybe I'll get there eventually," I tell him, closing my eyes. "But for now, I just want to forget all my reasons for having to write in the first place."

Though my eyes are closed, I can feel his stare on my face. He shifts on the bed and presses a lingering kiss to my forehead. I don't know how long he plans on staying tonight, but when he leaves, I want to be asleep. So I let my consciousness slip away from me, along with my worries. At least for the time being.

SEVENTEEN

Dear Everly,

Nicolai was gone when you woke up. You don't know how he left without you noticing, because you're usually a light sleeper. And it's probably a good thing, because with him here, you were able to sleep well for the first time in a long time. If you knew he was leaving, you would have stayed awake, telling yourself to relax and go back to sleep.

The trouble is, every time you close your eyes, you still see Vaughn hovering over you.

Mariah's knock on my bedroom door startles me. I shove my notebook under my pillow in time before she opens the door. When her face appears, it's taut with worry.

I sit up straighter. "What's wrong?"

She motions me forward with her hand. "Come look at this, mija."

I step out of my room, following her across the hall to

her own bedroom. She shuts the door tightly behind us. "I don't want Amma to hear," she whispers. The late afternoon light coming in through the window illuminates the tiny specks of dust floating around us. Mariah's bed is unmade, and piles of clean, unfolded laundry are on the floor next to the dresser.

She hands me a sheet of paper. I take it from her, my eyes scanning the words in front of me. It's our renewed lease, along with a notice that makes my stomach drop. I pin Mariah with my gaze. "They're raising our rent?"

She sits on the edge of her bed and drops her face into her hand. "An extra hundred dollars a month."

I drop the paper to the ground, ball my hands into fists, and then start folding the laundry on the floor out of stress. "Don't worry. We'll make it work somehow," I lie.

"I know. It's just scary." She sits on the edge of her bed and covers her face with her hands.

"I'll get a second job."

"But you barely have time for school with one job, mija," she reminds me. "That won't work long-term."

I pinch the bridge of my nose. There's no way we can afford a rent increase like this unless I drop school and get a second job. We're barely making ends meet as it is.

It feels like all my dreams are being ripped away from me. First getting pregnant, and now this. The worst part is that no matter how hard I try to do things differently than my mom, I keep being thrown right back into her mold. I know I'm partly responsible, but this feels out of my control.

My phone vibrates, and when I see that it's a text

from Vaughn, I immediately want to punch something. Or someone.

I'm outside.

As if I need any more stress right now.

I toss the holey blouse I'm holding in a pile off to the side for later mending. "I'll be right back, Mom," I mutter.

"Where are you going?"

"I just need to lie down for a minute."

I go back to my room and shut the door before I text Vaughn back. *Drive off a bridge.*

I'm already gone. I just dropped something off on your doorstep as an apology for last night. Just tell that douchebag friend of yours to leave me alone. I swear, I won't mess up again. I promise.

I frown at his message. What the fuck is he talking about? I open the door and walk down the hallway to the living room. I peek out the window, lifting the cheap plastic blinds, to make sure Vaughn isn't standing on the other side.

All I see is a white box, so I open the door. I pick up the box. There's a picture of a smartwatch on the cover.

What the hell is this, Vaughn? I write.

An apology.

I roll my eyes. If he thinks a fucking present could change anything, he's even more of an idiot than I thought. *You're lucky I still need your DNA. Otherwise I'd call the police and have you arrested.*

Your friend said the same thing. I won't touch you again. Just tell him to leave me the hell alone.

My friend? *Are you talking about Nicolai?*

Yes.

I turn off the screen. I don't know what Nicolai said or did to Vaughn, but if whatever it was is enough to keep him away from me from now on, I'll be amazed.

I take the smartwatch to my room and toss it on the bed. When I go back to Mariah's room, she's still sitting on her bed. She has the phone pressed to her ear. There's a troubled expression on her face. "Please, Ma," she says. "I hate to ask, but I need the money."

I close my eyes. This isn't the first time we've had to ask my grandparents for money. I hate it, especially since doing so will only offer us temporary reprieve.

"I know, I know." She grips the phone in both hands like it's a lifeline and she's about to drown. "I'm going to work extra shifts. I have to anyway, because Everly is taking more classes in September and won't be able to work as much."

I'm grateful Mariah is such a supporter of me going to college, but there has to be some way I can help. I could get another job temporarily, but I have a feeling if I were to see extra money coming in, it would be hard to part with when the time came to let it go next semester.

Mariah is right about me continuing my education. I'll just have to get through this pregnancy speedbump and get the damn degree that will earn me a living wage. And in the meantime, find a way to make more money on the side. Until the baby, at least.

"Thank you, Mama," she says, sagging in relief. She places a hand to her chest. "I'm so sorry for asking, but thank you, thank you."

I exit her room and close the door. I walk down the hall, stopping halfway through to stare at the watch on my bed through the open doorway. I'm glad my grandparents are well-off enough that giving us money isn't going to put them terribly under, but it's not like they're living in the lap of luxury. They can't keep helping us forever.

We used to live with them but moved out when Mariah and Chris got married. Having them nearby was a constant reminder that it wasn't only me and Mariah. That we had other family who cared about us and were there for us to lean on.

I try to picture Grandpa's face, the way his salt and pepper hair stood out against his dark brown skin. Him kissing Abuela on the cheek and cackling at my attempt at a disgusted expression whenever they showed affection.

Chris made a decent living and still pays child support for Amma, but after he left, Mariah couldn't bear to sacrifice her independence and move back home. Part of me still wonders if life would be easier for us if we'd sucked it up and gone back to them. At least we could all help each other.

"Ooh," says Amma behind me. I turn and catch her peering into my bedroom. "What's that?"

She's looking at the white box containing the smartwatch Vaughn gave me. My cheeks burn. "What's what?"

Amma walks right over to it and picks it up. "You got an Apple Watch?" she says, eyes round in wonder. "How?"

"It was a gift."

She gapes at me. "Pretty expensive gift."

"I know. At least four hundred bucks." I don't know

why Vaughn felt so compelled to buy me something I don't even need, or want. I would have rather he paid my rent.

And then the thought expands.

"You're a genius, Amma." I take the box from her, scan the details, and then list the watch for sale on every online platform I can access.

Four hundred dollars. Four months of raised rent, paid. I shut off my phone, even though I want to gaze at the screen impatiently for someone to contact me about the watch.

Instead, I open my notebook and write:

Dear Everly,

Maybe hope doesn't have any protection of its own because hope, real and true hope, is strong enough on its own to withstand any needle that threatens to pierce it.

Maybe hope doesn't have protection because it's the one doing the protecting.

A few days after I list the smartwatch, something bizarre happens. Chris arrives to pick up Amma for visitation.

It's weird seeing this man who hardly ever comes around, who has almost become a stranger. Seeing his tan face, his dark hair, and the familiar birthmark under his right ear is like watching an old home video I thought I forgot about.

"How are things, Everly?" he asks. He leans

awkwardly against a wall in the living room, like he's afraid to sit down. He also looks at me out of the corner of his hazel eyes, as if facing me like a normal person is too much of a commitment.

"Things? You mean life?" I ask blandly. "Expensive. Life is expensive."

"You're telling me."

As if he has anything to worry about. He isn't supporting a family of three on jobs that pay shit. I know for a fact his parents still support him; they're the ones paying Amma's Saint Mary's tuition.

"Yes." I glare at him. "I'm telling you." I don't care if I'm being rude. He left Mom when Amma was still a baby. He's the reason I was forced to homeschool myself so I could take care of her. Everyone else seems to have forgiven him except me. Maybe I'm the only one who sees him as the deadbeat piece of shit he is.

He clears his throat awkwardly, but Amma comes to his rescue, emerging from the room she shares with Mom. She's wearing jeans and a pink hoodie, and her crossbody bag is slung over her shoulder.

Chris raises his eyebrows. "Why do you have your mom's purse, sweetie?"

"What do you mean?" Amma tilts her head sideways. "This is mine, Dad."

Chris reddens. "What do you need a purse for? You're six years old!"

"I'm seven."

I suppress a laugh at the baffled expression that crosses his face.

"That's too young to be carrying a handbag,

Amethyst. Leave it here." His tone is final and sends sparks of anger through me, especially when Amma's face falls, and she starts to take off the purse.

"If she's old enough to have belongings of her own, she's old enough to carry them around in a bag." The challenge in my voice is unmistakable. Part of me hopes Chris will get angrier, so all pretense of politeness will fall away, and I can tell him exactly what I think of his parenting. Or lack of it.

"I'll decide what's appropriate for my daughter, not you." The way he says it makes me want to laugh. Like he's entitled to pass judgment on Amma's life. As if making a few arbitrary decisions is all it takes to be a responsible parent.

"Oh, really? And how long until you make your next big decision? When you see her again in six months?"

"Stop," says Amma, clearly upset. It makes my blood boil. "I'll leave the bag. All I had in it was glitter slime and some snacks anyway."

Chris grins. "That's my girl. You can bring the slime, and you don't need snacks. We're going out to eat."

They walk to the door. I promised Mariah I'd be here to see Amma off while she was at work, and it was worth it. I'll take every chance I can to tell Chris just how shitty a dad I believe he is.

After they leave, I pull out my phone and scroll through Facebook. I remember what life used to be like when Mariah and Chris were still married. Oddly, he still has photos from that time on his profile. I search through the photos and stop at one of me on my eleventh birthday. Chris barbequed, and I had a silly smile on my face as I bit into the ribs he prepared.

A pang shoots through my chest at the memory. That was before Chris revealed his true colors to us.

A text from Nicolai comes through. *Hey. Just wanted to check and see how you're doing.*

I smile. *So considerate. I'm fine, Nico. Thanks. But I'm curious ... what did you do to Vaughn? He dropped a gift off at my place and promised to leave me alone.*

Showed him how it felt to be threatened. That's all. He didn't bother you, did he?

I imagine a variety of scenarios between Nicolai and Vaughn, trying to land on one that feels realistic enough to make sense of Vaughn's new attitude. But I come up empty. I type, *No. He didn't bother me this time.*

I put my phone down and get my notebook from my room. I could and should be working right now, but I have to stay here until Amma comes back so she won't be home alone after Chris drops her off in a couple hours. I write:

> *I long for the day when I lie sick in my bed*
> *when my mother waits by my head*
> *rubbing my skull into submission*
> *working through the trauma,*
> *the pain,*
> *the fever.*
> *When I can be a child,*
> *Yes, finally,*
> *For what feels like*
> *the first time.*

Though I'm not yet an adult
I haven't been a child in years.

I rest my head against the couch cushions and close my eyes.

The happy image of my eleven-year-old face is still imprinted on the back of my eyelids, and it both haunts and comforts me as I fall asleep.

EIGHTEEN

Dear Everly,

For the first time in your life, you've been avoiding going to church. It's not that you don't want to go. You do. Church is a place you love, a place where you can pray in peace. It's a place where you're reminded to count your blessings.

But lately, you're afraid to go. You feel guilty because you don't want to be pregnant, and having an abortion sounds so appealing. You want to make the right choice. You want to make God happy. But how are you supposed to go through with this when you're not ready?

When Chris first left, you were so angry at God, Everly. You thought he stopped listening to your prayers for a dad. But in the end, Chris leaving made you a stronger person. It helped you realize that a dad isn't a title, it's a job. And Chris wasn't the right person for it. Deep down, Everly, you knew that. You just didn't care.

once upon a time
you thought God stopped listening
stopped caring

stopped hearing
but deep inside
you had a
f e e l i n g
His voice, the one you called
you didn't want to hear
You refuse to make the same mistake twice, Everly. This time,
when God tells you something, you'll listen. All you need to figure out
is what exactly he's trying to tell you.

NINETEEN

I should have expected this, with my luck. I should have anticipated that all *three* men in my life would want to come to the paternity testing appointment.

Actually, that's a stretch, and gives Vaughn way too much credit. He has to be here because it's his DNA we're testing as well as John's. And—currently sandwiched between Vaughn and Nicolai—I'm kicking myself for not being more mentally prepared for this outing.

John is sitting on Nicolai's other side, and Vaughn keeps glaring at him over my lap. There are three other couples in the waiting room, and I could die of embarrassment merely from the looks they're giving me.

"Why the hell is he here anyway?" Vaughn demands, his eyes cold and hard on Nicolai. I still don't know exactly what went down between them when Nicolai went into the salon to get my keys. But that aside, after being decked by Nicolai the first time they met, I guess I can understand Vaughn's animosity.

"I told you," Nicolai says easily. "I'm the one the doctor *thinks* is the baby's father because I was here for Ev's first ultrasound." He throws his arm around my shoulder. "Technically, it makes the most sense for me to be here."

"I have to admit, Everly," says John solemnly, leaning over Nicolai to look at me, "I'm a little disappointed I wasn't invited to that."

"I'm not," Vaughn murmurs. "Babies give me the creeps."

I stare at him numbly for a moment before turning back to John. "I didn't want the doctor to judge me, and it wouldn't make sense to invite you without inviting Vaughn. What if it's his baby?"

John looks somewhat mollified by my apology. "I understand. But in the future—"

"If the baby is yours, which we'll know in a week, obviously you'll be invited to everything." It's impossible to hide the irritation in my voice, but I'm not sure what he expects. It's not like I'll keep pretending Nicolai is the baby's dad after I know the truth.

Nicolai clears his throat and looks away, and I feel an ache in my heart. Discussing the future in front of him is more uncomfortable than I expected. With Vaughn, it's no problem, because there is no future. But with John … there's really no reason for there not to be one, other than our age difference. But that's more of an unchangeable technicality than a real hurdle to overcome.

A nurse calls my name. She gives our group a look of surprise but otherwise doesn't say anything else. The men loiter awkwardly in the hall while the nurse takes my blood pressure and temperature, then directs us to the exam room.

"The doctor will be with you shortly," she says and closes the door.

Vaughn sits in the only chair, the jerk, so I lean against the wall.

"Get up," says Nicolai, looking disgusted. "Let Everly sit down."

I appreciate him calling Vaughn out, but this isn't the place for confrontation. The last thing I need is for Vaughn to blow up and get us escorted out of the office. "I'm fine, Nicolai."

Vaughn smirks and leans back in the chair, making an obvious show of getting comfortable. John sighs and stands stiffly across from me, arms crossed in annoyance. He stares at the linoleum floor, his muted blue eyes far away and melancholy. He looks young—obviously, being in his early thirties—but the expression on his face makes him look so incredibly old.

Vaughn rests his chin on his chest. The fluorescent lights in the room shine on the short strands of his dark hair. "God, I hope it's not mine," he says in a rush of exhalation.

Nicolai clenches his hands. "How can you say that?"

"Bro," Vaughn says, looking up to glare at Nicolai, "do you want a screaming baby running around? With stinky diapers and shit? I don't think so."

"First of all," Nicolai says. "Babies don't run around. They're *babies.* And yes I would. They're adorable." His eyes meet mine, and my heart flutters.

"Dude, what are you going to do if it's yours?" Vaughn asks John.

John half smiles, the tiniest bit of sadness leaving his face. "Marry Everly, of course. We'll take care of the child together."

The room is silent, and a wave of embarrassment envelops my entire body. *Marry me? Seriously? You can't just say that like it's nothing!*

I risk a glance at Nicolai, and he's staring hard back at me. My stomach feels heavy, and I drop my eyes to the floor, unsure of what to say. I hope the doctor walks in soon.

"Does Everly get a say in that?" Nicolai finally asks. "The marriage part?"

John says, "It's the right thing to do."

I'm about to ask how he could possibly know that when Dr. Norman comes in. "Hello, everyone. I see we have a full house today!"

I grimace. "Yes. I'm DNA testing two of them." I gesture to Vaughn and John. "And you remember Nicolai."

Dr. Norman's eyes twinkle. "So it wasn't a friend you were asking questions for? I had a feeling." She scans her chart. "You want to do non-invasive paternity testing? All we need is a quick cheek swab from each paternal candidate and a blood draw from you, my dear. The good news is that since we're doing non-invasive, you won't need a needle in your uterus, but in your arm. Your results will take about a week to process. When they come in, we'll give you a call."

I smile as best I can, though I'm so nervous my hands shake. I hold out my arm. "Whenever you're ready." But all I can think is, *Just do it. Do it already.*

Test the blood in my veins.

Tell me who I—who we—belong to.

Vaughn leaves after his cheek is swabbed, but John and Nicolai stay until the end of the appointment.

John places his hand on my back as we walk out to the parking lot, guiding me toward his car, since I came here with him. My eyes meet Nicolai's, and my heart falters at his resigned expression.

I hesitate, then stop. "If it's all right, I think I'll have Nicolai take me home." John's eyebrows pull together. "But here. You can have this." I hand him the ultrasound photo from today, which he takes gently. It's the least I can do. His face looks so pitiful that I can't help but worry I've ruined this entire outing somehow. Like maybe he expected us to drive back to his place as a "family" and discuss the marriage thing.

All the more reason to ride with Nicolai. I'm not sure there's anything I could say to John that would actually make him happy.

His eyes linger on the photo, shining with reined-in emotion. "Thank you," he says simply.

I tell him I'll be in touch soon and say goodbye.
Nicolai and I get in his car and my spirits lift
significantly.

"That was hell," I state.

He laughs. "Which part? Because I had a great time."

I shake my head. "Don't even."

Through the window, as Nicolai drives to my part of
town, I watch elaborate homes become townhouses, and
townhouses shift into run-down apartment complexes. It's
depressing, despite the lightness I feel from being in the
car with Nicolai.

He parks in the guest spot at my apartment, and I
turn to him. "Would you like to come in?" There's a lilt to
my voice I can't suppress. Being near him is like drinking
coffee for the first time; energizing and optimistic. It
makes me feel full of possibilities.

He smiles. "Yeah. Sure."

We make our way upstairs and inside. Mariah has the
car, because she's off early today, and will be picking
Amma up from school soon. So, it's just us.

Alone, in the apartment.

"This is it," I say, gesturing to the plainly furnished
space. "In the daytime, at least. Home sweet home." My
cheeks burn when I look around, seeing what he must
see now that he has a chance to actually look: peeling
paint, unmatched furniture with worn holes in the
upholstery, carpets stained by the tenants who lived here
before us.

"I know. I've been here before."

"Only briefly, though." I fiddle with the ends of my
hair nervously.

He sits on the sofa and comments on the only thing I'm not currently assessing. "It's a little dark in here."

Add that to the list, Everly. No fucking electricity.

I cringe. "Yeah, sorry. I would turn the light on, but the power was shut off. No TV either, and we're eating a lot of pasta and peanut butter."

He presses his lips together. After a moment, he says, "Can I see your room?" With a smile, he adds, "In the daytime?"

"Sure." There's nothing embarrassing there, other than my notebook, which is well-hidden in my underwear drawer. But for some reason, the idea of him being in my space makes my blood rush, like I stood up too quickly. "Sure. This way."

He follows me down the hall and into my bedroom. White walls, brown carpet, and a yellow quilt on my bed. He sits on the mattress and bounces a little. It reminds me of the way I bounced on John's bed when I saw it the first time. I'm surprised to find that memory is melancholy.

I sit beside Nicolai and listen to him breathe.

"I didn't like the way he talked about you today," he says.

"Who, Vaughn? It's not a big deal. He's always like that."

He shakes his head. "Not Vaughn. *John.* He spoke of marrying you as if it was your only option."

My shoulders drop. "I don't really have a choice, though, do I, Nico? Isn't he right about that being the best thing?"

His eyes look more green than blue right now, and they sear through me with enough intensity to set a fire.

"The right thing," he says evenly, "is to follow your heart."

If only he knew how much I wish I could be selfish enough to do something like that. And if only he knew how he makes my heart react when he looks at me.

I glance at my underwear drawer, fingers itching for my notebook. But now's not the time.

I lean toward him until I can't take it anymore and press my lips softly against his. He cradles my face, and blood roars in my ears.

What am I doing? You shouldn't be kissing Nicolai. Stop, Everly!

But all rational thought has fled, and I'm pulling him on top of me as I fall on the bed. He grunts into my mouth and I kiss him more urgently. He kisses me back, withholding nothing, and I give in to getting what I want, what I need.

This is what it's like to really be kissed. To be kissed like I'm wanted.

I pull his shirt off over his head, and he removes my tank top. He looks me over, and his pupils dilate.

I reach under the waistband of his pants, wanting him ferociously.

"Ev." He shuts his eyes, clearly at war with himself. "We shouldn't."

I nod. "Okay." I remove my hands and start to pull away, but he grunts in exasperation and lowers himself against me. He kisses my neck and heat travels from his lips on my skin all the way to the place between my legs.

I hear the sound of the front door unlocking. "Shit!

What time is it?" I glance at my nightstand; the clock reads 3:30 p.m.

Mariah is here with Amma. I shove him off me and throw his shirt at him. "Get dressed, my mom and sister are home."

He swears and quickly dresses. I do the same, hoping and praying my lust for him isn't written on my face in permanent ink for them to see.

When we're both presentable, we exit my room just in time for Amma to walk through the front door behind Mariah. When they see Nicolai, they freeze.

Oh, God, kill me now.

"Hi," Amma says hesitantly. "Are you the same guy from last time?"

"Amma!" Mariah widens her eyes at my sister. "That's rude." I want to laugh because she has no idea Amma has met Nicolai, and she's not implying anything offensive. She walks over and stretches out her hand to Nicolai. "I'm Mariah, Everly's mom. Nice to meet you."

"Nicolai." He grins and shakes her hand. I can tell that there's some effort behind his smile only because I've seen the genuine version before. He must be nervous.

"Nicolai is Simone's brother," I tell them, and their expressions shift from suspicion to recognition and curiosity. "He came by to get my key to their house because he accidentally locked himself out. He's leaving now."

"Nonsense," Mariah says cheerfully. "Nicolai, you have to stay for dinner. I've heard so much about you from Simone and your mother."

I narrow my eyes at him. *Do not say yes.*

"I'd love to," he says. He smirks and pulls out a chair at the table. "What are you making?"

She bites her lip, probably thinking of our empty and powerless fridge. "Well, to be honest, I might need to make a quick trip to the store."

"We'll go!" I grab his arm and yank him to his feet. "Text me the list." Anything to get him out of here.

"That wasn't funny, saying you'd stay," I say over my shoulder as Nicolai follows me inside the grocery store. The sun is going down, but he doesn't miss the glare I offer him.

He widens his eyes innocently. "What was I supposed to do? Tell your mom I didn't want to stay?"

"Yes." I spin around to let the full force of my irritation seep in. "That's exactly what you were supposed to do."

"But why?"

I zig-zag through customers to the deli. Since the power is out, we can't use the stove to make anything ourselves. Nicolai keeps up easily. "Do you want Simone to find out you stayed for dinner? It's one thing to stop by to get a spare key. Luckily, I have one from the last time your parents asked me to house-sit. But anything more might seem suspicious!"

"Okay, I hadn't thought of Simone." He touches my elbow. "I don't have to stay. I'll go right now if it makes things easier for you. For your friendship with my sister."

It's difficult to stay mad because I know my reasons

are weak. If Simone were the only obstacle, I'd tell her I like her brother today. But there's no future for me with Nicolai. Not while I'm pregnant with another man's child. Not when I still don't know which man is responsible for that.

I open my mouth to tell him to leave, but the words won't come out. Not with him looking at me like that, like he can see inside me. Not with the ghost of his lips still imprinted on my skin, and me still feverish with desperation for him.

"It's fine," I say. "You can stay for dinner." He presses his smile between his lips to keep it from showing, but not very well, because I can't help but laugh. "But if Simone finds out, it's all your fault."

"I'll take the blame gladly," he murmurs, inching his way closer to me. A man clears his throat as he walks around us.

"We're completely blocking the aisle. We have to move."

Nicolai steps aside to allow traffic and tucks a stray red curl back into place. "Is that better?"

I feel slightly dizzy. How is he able to do that to me with a simple touch? "Let's get what we need and get out of here."

"Nick?"

I look over. A tall, pretty Asian girl is a few feet away, holding a bag of coffee beans.

"Kiley!" He freezes and then releases me and hugs the girl. She bounces up and down and hugs him back, and I'm alarmed at the intense wave of jealousy that crashes through me. It's completely unwarranted; Nicolai just had to spend the day with the two prospective fathers of my baby. And he didn't complain once.

Who the hell is she?

And why do they look so damn happy to see each other?

"Are you back?" he asks.

Kiley shrugs, a huge grin on her face. "I'm back!"

He turns to me. "Everly, this is my best friend from forever ago, Kiley. Kiley, this is Everly, my sister's friend."

My sister's friend. Nice.

I shake her hand like a grownup, even though I want to pluck her long-ass eyelashes out one at a time. "Nice to meet you."

She smiles with no trace of animosity, annoying me even more.

"How was New Zealand?" he asks. "Why did you leave?"

"It was great but kind of lonely, to be honest. There's no place like home. We can catch up later." Her attention briefly flicks to me. "I just had to say hi when I saw you."

"For sure. Let me get your new number." Nicolai pulls out his phone, and before I let my jealousy show, I move to the display of hot, pre-made foods.

I scan the different options, but I hardly register any of them. I'm listening to Nicolai talking to Kiley like seeing her has made his entire day.

Not like it matters. He and I are just friends.

A few minutes later, Kiley waves goodbye, and Nicolai joins me. I glance at him and find the remains of his smile from his earlier conversation are still on his lips. I suppress a large eye-roll.

"I'm getting an order of chicken wings, some potato wedges, and a pasta salad." Fuck. I sound bitter. And bitchy.

Nicolai asks, "Are you okay?"

"Yeah. Just hungry."

TWENTY

Nicolai and I bring the food in with one trip. The sun has set, so the house is completely dark without electricity, but Mariah has lit several candles and placed them throughout the apartment. The flames dance, casting moving shadows along the walls. The way they sway is poetic. It makes my fingers itch for my journal.

I place the grocery bags on the counter with a thud and my mom turns from where she's washing dishes at the sink. She smiles. "Thank you, mija."

I turn around and find Nicolai watching Amma, hard at work on her homework on the table and squinting through the dismal lighting.

"Whatcha working on?" he asks her.

"History assignment. I'm definitely going to fail, just so you know," Amma states matter-of-factly.

He laughs. "Why do you say that?"

Amma glances at him with a resigned expression.

"History is my worst subject. I'm no good at remembering dates, and neither is Everly or Mom."

He rubs the back of his neck. "Well, that does sound difficult."

Amma nods and turns back to her homework.

"But what if I told you that history is just the world's longest, most unbelievable, craziest story of all time?"

Amma shrugs. "I guess that would make it more interesting."

"That's all it is, really." His voice has become animated, lit with enthusiasm that can only be a product of passion. "It's a story. An interesting, important story."

Amma laughs. "Stories aren't important."

"But they are," he insists. "Stories are the most important and underrated things in the world. Without stories, we would only be facts and actions. There would be no meaning behind anything."

"I guess. Can you help me with my homework since you seem to care so much about history?"

"Sure." He leans over her shoulder to read the question she's working on and says something to her, but I'm not listening anymore.

I watch the way his face lights up as they talk, how he listens to her and then responds as if she's an adult.

I realize I've never seen a man interact with Amma since Chris was around. Chris still treats Amma like a baby, even though she's clearly growing up. Some people have a real knack for talking to kids, and Nicolai is one of them. A natural. No wonder he wants to teach, and I can tell he'll be good at it. Probably a great father someday, too.

The idea of him having kids someday with someone else sends powerful sparks of jealousy through me.

I quickly walk to the kitchen. Mariah is almost finished putting all the food on plates for everyone. "Need any help?"

"No. I'm done. See?"

I nod.

"He seems nice." She jerks her chin in Nicolai's direction. "And handsome."

"Mom!" I lower my voice. "He's Simone's brother."

"That means he isn't allowed to be nice or handsome?"

I blush. "I'm going to change. These clothes are uncomfortable."

I rush down the hallway until I'm safe in the confines of my room. I change out of my jeans and cringe at the impression they've made on my skin under my belly button. Fantastic. Like I have money lying around to buy new clothes. I open my dresser and grab a pair of leggings. These might even fit 'til the third trimester.

When I finish changing, I release my hair from its low ponytail and twist a few limp pieces around my finger to reshape them.

My phone vibrates. It's a message from Leland.

Hi, Everly. Wow. Mariah is your mom? I haven't heard from her in years. I'd love to meet you. I'm free tomorrow. Does that work?

My heart stops.

Leland wants to meet me? Tomorrow?

I know I should be excited at the idea of finally getting answers but I'm terrified, because if this man is the same one Mariah claims has been dead since before I was born, that makes her a liar. There is nothing more frightening to me than the idea of my own mother keeping secrets of this magnitude from me.

Kinda like people who hide their pregnancy. I wince with guilt, but shake it off. Unlike Mariah, I have plans to tell her. I'm just waiting for the right time.

I leave my room without responding to him. Mariah is laying out utensils next to the plates of food on the table. Nicolai is sitting across from Amma, and I take the empty chair next to him. I wonder if he can somehow see the conflict churning within me. But I can't tell him what's on my mind. Not with Mariah and Amma close enough to hear.

When Mariah says grace, Nicolai threads his fingers through mine underneath the table.

"I'm starving," says Amma when Mariah's done, setting down a pink blob and picking up her fork.

"No way." Nicolai gestures to the blob. "Is that homemade glitter slime?"

Amma beams proudly. "Made it myself."

He grins. "May I?" Amma nods, and Nicolai squeezes the slime, kneading it between his hands like dough. "This is incredible."

I smother a laugh. "How the hell do you know what that is? What, are you five?"

"I've been trying to think of some neat gifts to give the middle schoolers for acing tests," he explains. "But glitter slime isn't nearly as easy to make as the directions promised."

"It wasn't hard at all," says Amma. "I can show you how I make it sometime."

Nicolai sets the slime back down. "I'm going to hold you to that."

"Are you a teacher?" Mariah asks.

"I got back from college a few months ago, and I'm starting a student teaching program soon."

A dreamy look enters Mariah's eyes. "I always wanted to be a teacher, but after I had Everly, there wasn't much time for college." Her lips form a tight smile.

He looks confused, so I fill him in. "She had me when she was still in high school."

"Ah," he says, an easy grin forming on his lips. "That's why you look so youthful, Ms. Martin."

She laughs. "Please, call me Mariah."

I roll my eyes at how charming he is and eat a forkful of pasta salad. As soon as it's in my mouth, the texture makes me gag. I try to hide my disgust as I swallow it down. My stomach churns, but I try to ignore it. I inhale sharply through my nose, but it feels like I just sat down after spinning too fast. Acid shoots up my throat.

No, no, no, no, no.

I run for the bathroom.

Mariah stands up. "Everly?"

I ignore her and run to the toilet, almost missing it in the dark as I vomit up everything in my stomach. I steady myself with a few deep breaths and hope that's the last of it. I stand slowly, weakly, and make my way back to the table, where everyone has grown silent.

The short flames on the candles illuminate Mariah and Amma, watching me in confusion. I've been hiding this pregnancy from Mariah for almost three months now but somehow she's remained oblivious to all the signs.

Only Nicolai's face is knowing, and there's deep concern in his eyes. "You all right?"

"I'm fine. I probably caught a bug." I want nothing more than to go lie down, but I don't want to leave him alone out here. So I say, "Could I talk to you in private for a minute?"

He follows me to my room, and Mariah tells Amma to finish eating. I hear the scraping of their forks against the plates as we enter my room. I pull back my blankets and get in. Nicolai sits on the edge, looking worried. "You still haven't told them you're pregnant?"

"I'm going to," I state. "Soon."

"When?"

"When I know who the dad is."

Nicolai releases a frustrated sigh. "Everly—"

"That's only a week from now. One week."

"And then what?"

"What do you mean?"

"What happens to us when you find out? I go back to being Simone's brother while you walk off into the sunset with your baby daddy?"

I snort. "Yeah, right. Vaughn would sooner push me off a cliff than do that. He wants me to get rid of the baby. He won't try to make things work."

Nicolai is silent for a long moment. "But John would."

I'm unable to meet his eyes. So I stare at his hands instead. "Yes. John would."

He touches my chin, moving my face so I'm forced to meet his eyes. "And you? Would you want to make it work with him?"

I don't know what to say. Part of me wishes I'd never met Nicolai. Never gone on that stupid, accidental date with him, because then things wouldn't be so fucking complicated. I could tell him yes, that of course I would make things work with John, who has always wanted kids and has more money than he can count. He's kind and thoughtful, but also quite possibly depressed. And maybe having a child would actually make him happy. Give him a reason to live again.

Then there's Nicolai. Nicolai, who is also kind and caring. Not rich, but a genuine person who makes me laugh and not feel so alone in this miserable life of mine. The brother of my friend.

My friend.

"I don't know," I finally tell him. "I'm just so confused." My vision blurs, but I blink back the tears before they can fall.

"Ev," he says. He pinches the bridge of his straight nose. "I thought I could sit back and be your friend. Watch you marry someone like John, or even Vaughn, as long as it makes you happy. But I was wrong. I can't do this."

"Why not?"

"Come on, Everly." His voice is strained. "What are we doing? A few hours ago, you were begging me to—" he cuts himself off. "We can't be friends. Not when I obviously have feelings for you."

The only light in my room comes from the streetlights, filtering in through my blinds to illuminate his face.

"Tell me there's a chance you'll choose me even if John is the father. That wanting to be with you is not pointless." He lightly touches my face, his fingers leaving a trail of fire across my cheekbones.

"I'm sorry, Nico," I say, hating the way my voice breaks. The way my heart aches at the look in his eyes. "I can't promise you that. I have no idea how I'll feel after I know who the father of this child is."

His jaw flexes. He looks down at the blanket covering me. "Okay. At least you're being honest." He brushes the hair away from my face and stands. Swallows. "I should probably go. I'll thank your mom for having me."

I nod. I hate myself more and more with each second that passes without me telling him to wait, that there is a chance I'd choose him, even though he's not the father of my child. That having him in my life is worth the risk of my baby's life being tainted by not having their parents together, the same way mine was.

He walks out the door, taking a little piece of me with him.

And I don't even want it back.

I stare at the closed door for a long time, eventually taking my notebook out of the drawer. I take my time as I write:

no wonder I'm drawn to your warmth
you send heat through my veins
like the sun
but that doesn't make you responsible
for helping me
g r o w.

The next morning, I have several messages from people interested in buying the smartwatch. I message the person with the highest offer, letting them know I can ship it to them as soon as I receive payment.

Just a little longer without electricity.

I get out of bed, cautiously, so as not to disturb my stomach. To my relief, I'm not nauseous. I might even be able to eat today.

I shuffle to the kitchen, bypassing the bathroom so I don't think of how I got sick last night. Or of Nicolai sitting on my bed afterward, telling me to choose him.

I drink a box of apple juice and pour myself a bowl of cereal with no milk. There's no time to get fancy. I have to take Mariah and Amma to work and school if I don't want to be stranded at home without a car. It's Monday, so the salon is closed, and I have the day off.

I'm supposed to meet Leland today.

It's a bittersweet thing, because I'm excited to learn more about this mystery man who might be my dad, but I'm also sad at the way last night ended. I know Nicolai is ignoring me. He hasn't responded to my texts, and I want to tell him about Leland.

But he's right. It's not fair to keep stringing him along or expecting him to treat me like a platonic friend when we both know there's more between us than that.

"Morning, mija," Mariah says, rushing into the kitchen to get her cup of instant coffee.

"Morning." I raise my juice box at her.

"Again?" She offers me a quizzical smile. "You haven't had coffee in weeks!"

Because I'm pregnant, and caffeine isn't good for the baby. "I've been sleeping much better at night without it."

She looks at me like I just told her I hate puppies and gulps hers down black.

Amma appears from the bathroom, wearing her school uniform. "The lights are back on," she announces.

I exchange a confused glance with Mariah. "What is she talking about? Did you pay the light bill?"

She frowns. "No. We don't have enough now that the rent got raised. It's either food or lights."

I flip on a light switch and brightness fills the room. "What the hell?"

Amma looks worried. "I don't get it. Isn't this a good thing?"

"Yes, but it doesn't make sense," I mutter. "No one paid the bill."

Unless …

I recall Nicolai commenting on how dark it was inside and me explaining why. He's the only other person who knew. I need to talk to him.

But first, I fetch my phone and text Simone. *Want to go to lunch later? I can pick you up this afternoon.* I've been planning to ask her if we can get together. I'm hoping she'll finally be ready to tell me about her mother's affair. If I go over there after meeting Leland, maybe I'll also have a chance to ask Nicolai if he had anything to do with this.

She replies instantly. *Ok! Can we have a full girls' day? I want to spoil you! Consider it a new mom gift!*

Her response makes warmth flood my heart.

"Well, I'm not going to question it!" Mariah smiles at the illuminated bulbs above her and holds her hands up. "I'm just going to enjoy it and thank the Lord!"

"Good idea, Mom. Now let's go, before you're late to work. Got to keep your job so the lights *stay* on."

After I drop them off, I park at the coffee shop where I'm supposed to meet Leland. It's a hole-in-the-wall place downtown that I've never been to; a place he suggested. I glance at my reflection in the mirror.

This is it, Everly. This is the day you might meet your dad.

I wonder what his first impression of me will be. I wonder if he has any idea that I could be his daughter.

A terrible thought occurs to me. What if the reason Mariah told me he died was because he didn't want to know me? And by telling me he passed away, she was eliminating the possibility that I'd try to find him?

A variety of terrifying yet entirely possible scenarios begin to plague my mind, making sweat drip down the back of my neck. I mentally berate myself into making them stop. I'm probably being ridiculous, but I'm still nervous as I make my way inside the small, brightly lit coffee shop. There's a long counter along the left wall with bar stools, and several empty tables sprinkled throughout the area. I look around for Leland, but he isn't here yet, so I pick out a table in the back and sit down.

As I look over the menu, I seriously consider leaving.

This might be a terrible mistake. I've never known Mariah to lie to me before. If she did lie about this, there's probably a good reason. Leland could be a dangerous man.

There's a receipt on the table. A pen, too. It's a sign to write a poem. At least, that's what I tell myself. I scribble down:

surround me with love
happiness
the salt of the
earth
so i can
t a s t e
what's good
if indeed
there is any good left

I add a few extra swirls to the paper, going over the letters until enough time has passed to convince me I shouldn't have come, that I'm being stood up. I pick up my phone and the receipt and scoot my chair back. It makes a loud noise across the floor.

"Everly?"

I glance up at the man standing next to the table. "Leland?"

He smiles and lowers himself into the chair across from me. It strikes me how handsome he is: dark skin with a stubbled mouth, warm brown eyes, and a nose ring. He looks the same as his online photo, but he's dressed in business slacks and a collared shirt.

"It's nice to meet you," he says. "I haven't heard from your mom in years. How's she doing?"

He seems so relaxed. Is it possible he thinks I asked him to come for a completely different reason? "She's fine. It's nice to meet you, too."

We sit in silence. The moment stretches out awkwardly. It's clear neither of us knows what to say next. Leland clears his throat.

"You dated my mom," I blurt out. I would much rather get straight to the point than sit here quietly a moment longer. "In high school, right?"

"For a little while." He frowns. "Is that what this is about?"

"Sort of." I'm nervous. My mouth goes dry, and I feel sweat trickle down my lower back. But I have to get to the bottom of this. I need to know the truth. "My mother told me my father died, that he passed away before she could tell him she was pregnant. But he wasn't her boyfriend."

Leland nods solemnly. "She had quite a few of those."

"She did?" I'm stunned. For some reason I find that hard to believe. After Chris, I've always known her to be single. Dedicated to me and Amma and church.

"From what I recall." Leland clears his throat. "She used to make me so jealous, especially when she dated guys who didn't go to school with us. Not to talk badly about her, of course."

I smile politely, but I didn't come to hear about my mom's teenage love life. "She told me my father's name was Leland Jones."

Leland frowns, as if he's beginning to understand. "And you think she was talking about me?"

I shrug, hope building in my chest. "You guys dated, and that's your name. 'Leland' isn't exactly common."

"That's true." He searches my face. He's confused, curious, and—to my dismay—apologetic. "I'm sorry, but I don't think your mom was telling you the truth, unless she's talking about someone else with the same name as me."

Anger builds inside me. Of course his first instinct would be to deny this. To refuse to accept any responsibility. "How can you say that?" I demand. "You're just *so sure* she's wrong?"

Leland looks taken aback at the drastic change in my demeanor. Gone is the kind, eager Everly, replaced by someone who has been burned too many times to count.

He looks more concerned than offended. "I'm sure, because your mom was saving herself for marriage when we were together."

"You mean ..."

He nods. "We never had sex."

"Oh, my God." I stand, purse in hand.

He doesn't try to stop me. "I'm sorry," he calls as I rush past him and out the door. I throw myself into the car, breathing heavily.

She lied. There is a tremendous weight on my chest, and I struggle to breathe. *She lied, she lied, she lied.*

I force myself to calm down, counting backward from twenty. I repeat this until I can no longer see sparkles at the edges of my vision.

I'm so embarrassed. Leland probably thinks I'm some

kind of deranged child. Some desperate, confused nutcase. There is no part of me that wants my own child to experience this. This loss of identity. It strikes me that this feeling is all too familiar, and it's the root of my turmoil about staying with John if he's the father.

TWENTY-ONE

I park on the street outside Nicolai's house.

Simone's house, I mentally correct myself. *Your loyalties lie with Simone.*

I retrieve my phone and numbly type:

we wish to make humans out of animals
in movies
in our minds
in our hearts
animating them, clothing them
forcing words of humor from their slick lips
wishing for them
humanity
when we don't even
know
what humanity is
you're an animal, they say
but i ask, what's an animal

they tell me an animal kills what's alive,
eats without heart
to survive,
makes a mess of things
they have no humanity
but i ask you
i ask you
i ask
who are the humans
and
who
are
the
animals?

Writing helps. It always does.

I knock on the front door, and Mrs. Beckett opens it. "Come on in, Everly. Simone is getting ready upstairs, if you want to head up there."

I'm more than a little surprised to see her still here. She looks strained, less put together than usual. Her clothes are wrinkled and her hair looks unwashed. But I know better than to comment on any of it. "Okay. Thanks."

I go up quietly. My goal is to stop at Nicolai's room before Simone realizes I'm here. I walk lightly, one step at a time. A few family pictures hang on the wall next to the stairs. Mr. and Mrs. Beckett, Simone, and Nicolai. Except these pictures are old, and Simone is just a baby. Nicolai is a young kid. I must have seen these photos dozens of times, but I still didn't realize who he was when I met him at Beanbags.

I'm halfway up when I hear Nicolai's voice behind me. "Hey, Ev."

I turn. "Hi. How are you?" I go back down the stairs until we're face to face.

He suppresses a smile. "Small talk? Really?"

"Well, what else am I supposed to do? Bare my soul on the stairs? I'm picking up Simone for lunch. It's our day off."

He's no longer smiling. His eyes are intense, blazing blue fire, and I feel it in my bones. "Have fun."

He starts to walk away, but I latch on to his arm. "Wait. I'm sorry." I want to tell him I met Leland and that he's not my dad after all. That I'm more lost than ever, and I want, *need*, his help. But I remember the reason I'm here. "I know you paid my mom's electric bill."

His eyes soften. "Okay."

"You weren't going to say anything?"

"I'm not looking for credit." His lips thin. "Just trying to help."

"I can't believe you would do that for me."

He laughs without humor. "You can't?"

"No."

He makes a frustrated sound. "I may not be as well off as John—"

"But that's why this means so much. Don't you see? To John this probably would have been nothing. But it can't be nothing to you. You haven't started working yet. Thank you, Nico."

He opens his mouth to say something as Simone

comes down the stairs. Instantly, we back away from each other before she can notice how close we're standing.

"Ready, girl?" she asks.

I paste a smile on my face. "Yep. Let's go!"

The restaurant isn't crowded, but I ask to be seated outside. I need to clear my head after that encounter with Nicolai, and it's a beautiful day; the sun is shining, but not too brightly to burn. A warm breeze lifts the hair off our necks and blows the smell of restaurant food into our faces. After skipping out on breakfast with Leland, I'm starving. We dig in when our meals arrive, and I try not to think of the way Nicolai looked at me, like the surface of a frozen lake about to crack.

"I'm glad you texted me," says Simone. She takes a bite of her taco. "I've missed you, Ever."

"Me too." We're at a new place in downtown Los Gatos that I've been wanting to try. Seeing Simone was the perfect excuse. Apparently, she's the perfect excuse for a lot of things these days. It makes my body taut with chagrin. "It seems like it's been forever."

"Way too long," she agrees.

"What's been going on lately?" I ask around a mouthful of French fries. "What's new with you?"

She hesitates, pressing a smile between her lips. "I'm seeing someone."

I drop the fry I'm holding. "What?"

"It's still new! I don't want to jinx it by talking about it."

I shake my head. "No way. You're not keeping the details from me. At least tell me her name."

"Relax. I'll tell you soon."

I pretend to pout, but I can't deny the small ache I feel at not being included. I can't remember the last time she didn't spill her love life to me as soon as a new interest blossomed. And then I realize how hypocritical that ache is. I'm doing the exact same thing.

"Speaking of telling," she says, "have you told your mom you're pregnant yet?"

I swallow a bite of food. "No, because I still don't know who the father is."

"When are you finding out?"

"The results come in at the end of this week or the beginning of next. I just want to find out and get it over with."

She props her head in her hands, elbows on the table. "Who are the options?"

Damn, have I really not told her? I can't believe it's been so long since we've genuinely talked and that so much has happened since then. "You know Vaughn?"

Her mouth falls open. "The Vaughn we *work with*?" I nod. She gapes at me. "When the hell did that happen?"

I don't want to tell her about the arrangement I made with Vaughn to keep my job. If she finds out, she'll report him, and the last thing I need is the possible father of my child going to jail. So, I say the most truthful thing I can, considering everything. "On my eighteenth birthday, before you and I went out."

"Are you guys, like, a thing? And who is the other man?"

"Vaughn and I are definitely not a thing, and the other man is named John. I met him at the bar after you left on my birthday."

Simone holds up a hand. "Seriously? Their names rhyme?"

"Weird, huh?"

"Who do you hope it is?"

"Definitely John. He has his shit together. He's a pediatrician. And he's nice. A little too old for me, but he wants to get married if the child is his."

Simone shakes her head, clearly overwhelmed. "Holy shit. And I thought my life has been complicated lately."

I jump on the change of subject. "What's been going on?"

A piece of straight, silky hair lifts off her face when she heaves a heavy sigh. "Just bullshit with my parents. My mom has been having an affair."

"Wow, really?" I try to sound like it's the first I'm hearing of it.

"Someone she met on the internet who's five years younger than her. Dad wants a divorce, but she wants the house and the landscaping business. Neither will budge. It's a mess."

"Oh, Simone, I'm so sorry." I lightly touch the back of her hand.

She smiles sadly. "Thanks."

"What do you think they'll end up doing?"

She brightens. "I'm going to propose that *I* take over the company, since they can't seem to agree with one another."

"I didn't know you wanted the company," I say, impressed.

"That's why I'm majoring in business, but it hurts, you know? Them being so selfish about all this. Nick is the golden child who got a scholarship. He's going to be a teacher. If they don't give me this, I'll have nothing."

I realize then that this has nothing to do with business. This is Simone's desire—no, *need*—to grasp control of an uncontrollable situation. A world that is suddenly falling apart around her.

I know the feeling all too well.

I reach across the table and squeeze her hand. "You don't really think they'll say no to you, do you?"

She shrugs. "They might."

It's hard to imagine Mr. and Mrs. Beckett fighting, let alone denying Simone. Every time I've seen them interact with her, it's obvious they're wrapped around her finger.

"They'll say yes. They will." My sure tone matches the way I feel, and I think some of my confidence transfers to her.

Her eyes shine, and she continues eating and gazing at pedestrians on the downtown strip. "You're right."

"Is there anything else bothering you?"

"Kind of. Nick seems different lately, but I don't know why."

"Different how?"

She ponders. "I don't know. He's always been happy, but lately he's been almost ecstatic. It's weird."

"Isn't that a good thing?"

"I guess so." She smiles faintly. "I just wish I knew why."

Simone is right; he's a genuinely happy person. He's more than that, though. He's kind and generous, and the one bright spot in my life, and a little part of me wonders if his being happier than normal has anything to do with me.

"You seem different lately, too," she says.

I frown at her, but all I can think is, *Shit. Please don't put it together.* "Different how?"

"Like you're in love. Are you?" She grins teasingly.

I pick at my food. "Not that I know of."

She smirks. "I know it isn't Vaughn, but how about John? He sounds pretty great."

Am I in love?

Is that what this is, this unbearable longing I feel for my best friend's brother? The way I want to be with him even after I've just seen him? How I want to tell him everything, even stupid things that don't matter? The way my heart flutters every time he looks at me with those gorgeous eyes of his or touches me, making my senses ignite and the pit of my stomach ache with a desperation I can hardly bear?

"He's no one," I say mechanically. "Or at least he's no one I can have."

Her eyes widen. "So you are in love. I knew it! But why can't you have him?"

"Because, I'm pregnant, and he's not one of the parental candidates. Simple as that."

"Who cares? If you want to be with him, be with him!"

"It's not that simple."

"Yes, it is," she insists. "I know you want to do the right thing for your baby. I get that you never had your dad in your life and always wanted that. But it would be unfair to your child if you married their father and stayed unhappy because you were in love with someone else. You might even end up getting divorced, which lots of kids agree is worse than never having their parents together at all."

I stare at her as her words sink in.

She's right.

She's totally right, but it scares me. Terrifies me. It would be so much easier to never tell Nicolai how I feel and run away with John, or struggle to co-parent with Vaughn, because it's what I feel I deserve. I don't have anything to offer Nicolai other than myself, and I don't know that I am enough.

It's so much easier to accept what I deserve than to get rejected for chasing what I want.

But at the end of the day, what's the risk? If I get rejected, I'll be right where I am now. If I don't try, I'll never know if I could have been happy.

"I think you should tell him," Simone says.

"I think I will."

"Good. Do you want to sleep over at my place tonight? Like old times?"

I stifle a laugh, trying to push thoughts of Nicolai away. I want to see him, of course. But spending time with Simone feels like wrapping my shivering body in a warm blanket. I've missed this. I've missed *her.* "I would love that." With a wry smile, I add, "You did say you wanted a full girls' day, remember?"

She claps. "We're going shopping and getting our nails done first. I want to buy you maternity clothes!"

"That's too expensive—"

"Stop it." She stifles my protests with a stern finger and an even more rigid glance. "I'm never having kids, so this is my only opportunity to buy stretchy but cute mom things. You will not take this from me. Besides, why waste a perfectly good day off?"

My too-tight jeans cut into my belly button, like they're agreeing with her. I sigh. "Okay then. Let's go."

Dear Everly,

There's a story in the Bible about an old widow who gave her only two coins at the temple in Jerusalem. Jesus proclaimed that she had given more than any other contributor, because though everyone else donated from their surplus of wealth, she had given her entire livelihood, all she had.

And Everly, you can't help but feel like the old widow.

While others have a surplus of wealth, nice families and clean pasts unmarred by mistakes, cars and stable jobs, security, and promising futures to give,

all you have is your heart.

Your measly two coins.

Those two coins are nothing
and everything.

The question is this: how do you, like the old widow, hand them over without fear?

I put my phone down and peek at Simone. We're

sitting in the theater, waiting for our movie to start. We're so early, the lights are still on.

Rather than talk to me, she's engrossed in texting whoever she's secretly dating. So I figure now is a good time to write some of my thoughts down.

I look at the entry I just wrote on my phone, thinking of Nicolai, and add:

Dear Everly,

You think Nicolai may be the old widow, too. Although he has much more than two coins to offer, he gives freely, without fear, and he gives more than he should.

You wonder if he's afraid of getting hurt. Probably not. He could pick up his broken pieces and offer them to someone new. No one would turn them down.

You, on the other hand? Your pieces have been broken so many times, they've turned to dust.

Maybe you were wrong about him being the old widow. He may be generous, but he still has plenty to give.

TWENTY-TWO

It's dark by the time Simone and I get back. Turns out that nails, new clothes, and seeing the latest horror film were exactly what we needed to feel like us again. Like best friends again.

I cringed at the amount of money everything cost, but Simone insisted on paying for it all as a "new mom gift" to me.

I giggle as she unlocks her front door. "I can't believe the knife was hidden in that music box the entire time, and literally *no one* thought to check it."

She nods. "Idiots."

We make our way inside the house and Simone flips on the lights. Nicolai rounds the corner from the kitchen, and our gazes lock, causing us both to freeze in place.

Simone, completely oblivious, tugs me past Nicolai. "Let's see if there's anything else scary to watch in my room."

A female laughs in the kitchen and Kiley appears, a

bright smile on her face. She's wearing a red bodysuit, and her long, dark hair is curled into a loose wave.

I feel like I might faint. What the hell is she doing here? Alone with Nicolai?

"Kiley! What are you doing here?" Simone says, echoing my thoughts. Her voice sounds uneasy.

Kiley bites her lip. "Just hanging with Nick." She casually puts an arm around Nicolai's shoulders.

Simone's tone hardens. "Oh."

Kiley stiffens. "I was just leaving."

Nicolai glances back and forth between his sister and Kiley, his eyebrows narrowing. I don't care what Simone's reasons are for talking to Kiley like she would rather see anyone else in the world. All I'm concerned with at the moment is why the hell Kiley is here with Nicolai.

Kiley walks out the front door, and Simone watches her the entire time. "Come on, Ever." She gestures toward the stairs again.

I nod numbly and follow Simone to her room.

We situate ourselves on her bed and start another movie, but neither of us is mentally present after seeing Kiley. I want to know what Simone has against her, but I can't ask because my heart is in my damn throat.

They were alone downstairs *in the freaking dark.*

That's not fair, I correct myself. *The kitchen light was on.*

I sink into Simone's mattress. When I glance over at her, taking in her peaceful and very asleep expression, I smile faintly. We're the only psychos I know who consider horror films appropriate bedtime stories.

I'm careful not to jostle the bed as I get up, so I don't

wake her, and move silently down the hall to Nicolai's room.

It's the same room I was in at his party. As soon as I enter, I'm reminded of when I was tangled in his arms.

He's staring out the window, his back to me. When I close the door, he turns, eyes narrowed at first, then softening ever so slightly as he takes me in. "What are you doing in here?"

"I came to talk to you."

He shakes his head. "Probably not a good idea."

"I don't care." I take a few steps toward him.

He sighs, unfolding his arms. "You can't keep doing this."

"Doing what?"

"Showing me what I can't have." The words are bare and unflinching. "I get it. You don't want to be with me. You and my little sister are best friends, and you need to keep your distance. But it's too damn hard to be near you without touching you."

"Is that why you called Kiley over tonight? To get over me?" I regret the words as soon as they leave my mouth.

Nicolai stares at me in disbelief. "Are you serious?"

"Why else was she here alone with you?"

"Kiley is my friend." His appalled expression makes my cheeks burn. "Just like you and Simone."

"Right. Your friend. Just like me and you." I turn to walk away. This was a bad idea. Telling Nicolai how I feel would only end in heartache. He was never meant to be anything more than Simone's brother to me, and it's my fault for letting things get this far. I should have put a stop to this as soon as I saw him at the party. I should have brought up the date right in front of Simone and laughed it off, landing him in the friend zone forever.

"Ev." His voice is gentle. "Talk to me."

"There's nothing else to say. You should be with Kiley, and I should be with whoever the hell the father of my child is."

He flexes his jaw. "Tell me the real reason you're here."

"It doesn't matter!" I practically shout. "I was being stupid."

He searches my face, then walks forward until he's close enough that I can feel the heat from his body. "Tell me."

I swallow. My heart is hammering. My temples are sweating. I'm so damn nervous and scared, and maybe that's why I've been pushing him away. Because other than my sister, I've never had a good thing in my entire life, and he's my first taste of it. Once I say it, there's no changing my mind.

"I choose you." My eyes meet his, and I whisper the rest before I can let my fear hold me back. "I want to be with you, Nico."

There's a beat of silence. Nicolai's gaze remains on mine, and for the briefest moment, I'm afraid he's going to ignore what I said, but then he lifts me in his arms and kisses me.

His lips are soft against mine, but with an urgency that sends panic and desire through me.

I gather two fistfuls of his thick golden hair and cling

to him, wrapping my legs around his waist, my heart pounding against his.

A thrill shoots through me at our closeness, our touch. I can't contain my desire, my attraction to him. Not just to his body but what's inside. His heart. His mind. All of him.

We stop kissing momentarily to undress. I'm down to thin panties and a violet lace bra that barely fits me because pregnancy has made my breasts swollen and round, and he stares.

"Get over here," he growls.

We're on the bed in an instant, and I lie on my back while he hovers over me. He kisses my lips first, then my chin, my neck, and my sensitive, swollen breasts. He pulls the lace of my bra away and kisses, sucks, licks until I squirm.

"Do you have any idea how long I've wanted to do this to you?" He kisses down my stomach, and when he's between my legs I have to bite down on a pillow to keep from waking the whole damn house. His expert tongue works until I see stars, and I do my best to muffle the sound of my climax with his pillow.

He brings his face back to mine. "I don't have a condom."

"I'm already pregnant," is my answer. And a moment later he's entering me, filling me. I groan and grip the bed sheets, meeting each of his thrusts with equal effort. His name escapes my lips through the pillow. Without it, I'd probably be yelling. He slows his rhythm to touch his forehead to mine.

Sex with Vaughn was nothing but trauma, blackmail,

and regret. Sex with John was my attempt to recover from the pain. Sex with Nicolai takes us from two distinct beings to one unique form: our skin touching everywhere, our hearts beating as one.

"I love you, Ev," he whispers against my mouth.

His thrusts become gentle and intense, pleasure and pain. He holds my hips, guiding our bodies together until he tenses with his release. I want the moment to stretch forever, to be consumed by him constantly, not an inch of air between us.

Our breathing slows. I lie facing him with my head resting on his right arm, and his left draped over me. The hand under my head plays with my hair. I don't dare utter a word, afraid of shattering this perfect moment, of destroying the illusion that everything can stay just like this, though I know morning will come like it always does.

I close my eyes, reveling in the sound of his heart against my ears, and fall asleep.

TWENTY-THREE

I open my eyes and squint against the panel of light filtering in through Nicolai's bedroom blinds. I yawn loudly, and he stirs next to me.

"Mm," he murmurs. He rolls so he's facing me, eyes still closed, and pulls me close.

He looks so peaceful. I can't help but smile. I'm tempted to trace the lines of his face with my fingertip, but I don't want to disturb him. I lean forward and kiss him ever so gently. His arm tightens around me.

"Nicolai?"

"Hm?" He squints at me through half-open lids.

"I met Leland Jones." I stare at the wall behind Nicolai, willing myself not to cry. "Turns out he's not my dad after all. He and my mom never had sex."

He touches my cheek. "We'll just have to keep looking. We got the wrong guy, Ev. That's all."

"I have a feeling there's more to it than that."

Someone rattles his doorknob. I glance over my

shoulder. Simone walks in, staring me right in the face while I'm in her brother's bed, his arm draped over my bare body.

Oh my God.

"What the hell is going on?" Simone asks. Her eyes are round and her lips are parted.

"What does it look like?" he says sleepily. He rubs his eyes, unfazed at being discovered.

"I can explain," I say to her.

"How long has this been going on?"

"It's kind of a long story. I'm sorry I didn't tell you." I rush to get the words out. "I didn't want to complicate things or make you feel like anything that happened between me and your brother would affect our friendship."

Simone briefly closes her eyes. "Wait a minute. Are you saying *he's* the other man? The one you love but isn't one of the baby daddies?" She turns to Nicolai. "You know she's pregnant, right?" She says it carefully, almost critically. Part of me feels stung that she blurted it out without hesitation. But the rest of me understands, because ultimately, Nicolai is her brother, and she's only looking out for him. Her loyalties lie with him.

The bed shifts as he sits up. He's wearing a bored and slightly annoyed look. "Yes, I know she's pregnant."

"And you told me I should go after the one I love," I remind her. "Yesterday at lunch, you said there was no reason I couldn't have him."

Simone grits her teeth. "That was before I knew you were talking about my *brother.*"

"I'm sorry. I should have told you about this when it started, the day I found out I was pregnant."

Her mouth falls open. "That's how long it's been? So you knew him at the welcome home party and didn't say anything?"

"I thought it might be awkward."

"No. This"—Simone gestures to the three of us—"*this* is awkward." She walks out of the room, closing the door loudly. The last thing I wanted to do was hurt Simone. She's been a good friend since the day I met her. She doesn't deserve this.

I face Nicolai. "Ouch."

"She'll get over it." He presses his lips together.

"What makes you so optimistic? She *has* to forgive you. You're her brother. Me, on the other hand—"

"You're my girlfriend. If she wants me to speak to her, she has to forgive you too."

I smirk. "Oh, really? How do you know I'm your girlfriend? I don't recall you asking."

He leans in to rub his nose along mine until my eyes fall closed. "Will you be my girlfriend, Everly?"

His sure tone, the way it doesn't sound like a question, makes me smile. "Yes."

He kisses me, and I sit on top of him, straddling his lap. I can feel how much he wants me again. He's not alone in his desires. I want him again, too, but I have a very angry best friend downstairs, and now is not the time.

I kiss the tip of his nose and then get up. I start putting my clothes on. "We should get dressed and explain things to your sister. I'll go down there first and talk to her while you dress."

He sighs. "Fine."

When I get downstairs, Simone is making a breakfast smoothie in the kitchen. She averts her gaze while I wait for her to finish blending. The moment seems to stretch out forever. When she finally turns off the blender, she pours some of the smoothie into a mason jar and turns to me. Well, sort of. Half her body is still facing the sink, like she doesn't want to look at me.

I wince. "Simone—"

"You don't need to explain, Everly. I get it. My brother is a total catch. I'm not upset that you like him."

I tilt my head. "Really?"

"Really." She sighs. "But what I don't understand is why you didn't just tell me."

"Come on, Simone! I mean, you didn't confide in me about your parents splitting up right away. Why? I kept texting you!"

She stares at the smoothie. "You have problems of your own. And I didn't want to talk to anyone, anyway. Besides, don't you realize how hypocritical you sound? You kept liking my *brother* from me!"

"Fine. You're right." My tongue feels numb, dead in my mouth. "It was because I've been in denial."

"What does that even mean?"

"I didn't *want* to like him, Simone." I wrap my arms around my torso. Stare at the beige tiles of the kitchen floor. "All this time, I've been hoping my baby is John's so I would have no obstacles being with him. I could just give my child the life I've always wanted."

"So basically, you couldn't commit to liking my brother," she clarifies. "You've kept Nick as a backup all this time, in case it's Vaughn who got you pregnant?"

I close my eyes. "That's not true. I still don't know who got me pregnant, but I want to be with your brother anyway." I lift my gaze, looking her straight in the eye. "I choose Nicolai, regardless."

She studies my face for a long moment. I don't know what she finds, but the tension in her shoulders relaxes. "You better not hurt him."

Relief loosens my limbs. "Thank you, Simone."

The corner of her mouth turns up, and Nicolai walks into the kitchen. He grabs me from behind, pulling me back against his chest. "You're not talking her out of being with me, sis."

"I doubt I could, even if I wanted to." She smirks, locking eyes with me. "I was just telling her I'm not angry."

"Good." He kisses my cheek.

"But now that you guys came clean, it's time I do too."

He stiffens. "What are you talking about?"

Simone sips her smoothie. "You know your good friend Kiley, Nick?"

"What about her?"

"Last night," Simone continues, "she wasn't here for you. She was here for me." A slow smile spreads across her lips. "She was using you as a cover to see me, and when I wasn't home, she waited. I was upset because I didn't want to risk you guys finding out we're together. That she came back from New Zealand for me. I was waiting to tell you until things got more serious."

"You're with Kiley?" I clarify.

She nods.

He chuckles in my ear. "Told you there was nothing to worry about with me and her."

"I feel like an idiot." I really do. "How did I not know, Simone?" Thinking back, it should have been obvious.

"Same reason I didn't know about you and Nick, I guess," she shrugs. "And the best part is, if you guys get married, we'll be sisters, Ever."

"Oh, shut up." I reach over and squeeze her hand. "We already are."

Nicolai and I go back upstairs after Simone leaves for work. I have a split shift with her later, but until then, I don't have anywhere else to be. And here in Nicolai's arms, wrapped in the warmth of his sheets, there's nowhere I'd rather be. He nuzzles his face into my hair, the way he always does when we lie down together.

My thoughts travel back to what Simone and I discussed before he came downstairs. "We should talk," I say.

"I'm all ears."

I pull my face away from his so I can look at him. "I might be having a baby." I bite my lip. "How does that make you feel?"

He thinks for a minute. "Other than being a little jealous that it's with another man, I'm really happy for you." He searches my face. "I think you'd be a great mom."

Great. Now I'm tearing up. I wasn't expecting him to compliment me. "You're okay with me raising someone else's child?"

"Why wouldn't I be?"

I shrug. "It might get complicated."

"You said you *might* be having a baby," he says. "Does that mean you might abort?"

"Only if it's Vaughn's," I say. "And even then, I probably won't. Depends on how I feel once I know, and if it's God's plan for me."

His eyes lock with mine and then travel down to my stomach. It's still flat, but harder than it usually is. "I'm okay with whatever you want to do." He takes my hand. "It's not up to anyone but you, Ev."

I bring his hand to my mouth, kissing it softly. "Thank you, Nico." I take a deep breath, letting my stress follow the exhale out of my body. I fish my phone out from under his pillow and check the time. "I have work at three," I say. "Do you have plans today?"

He starts to unravel himself from me. "I think we should go on a picnic."

A laugh bursts from my lips. "A picnic? Seriously?"

"Yes." He smirks. "Get changed and meet me downstairs."

I shake my head, trying not to smile but failing as Nicolai dresses in jeans and a black long sleeve. He gathers his wild hair into a bun and kisses my cheek before vanishing. His footsteps retreat down the stairs.

"A fucking picnic," I repeat to myself with a laugh.

Stretching, I get out of the bed. I slip into my new maternity jeans and make my way to the bathroom to check my hair. Thank goodness I know where Simone keeps her brushes and flat iron. I work quickly, braiding my hair and applying color to my lips, still swollen from kissing.

When I'm presentable, I take the stairs down to the kitchen, where Nicolai is putting two sandwiches into a—I kid you not—*picnic basket.*

"You're straight out of a fairy tale." Shaking my head, I laugh again.

He glances at me over his shoulder. "I made you a peanut butter and jelly sandwich. I hope that's all right. I read that pregnant women can't eat lunch meat because of the risk of listeria."

The smile on my face turns wobbly. And dammit, a knot forms in my throat. "You're going to make me cry."

His eyes widen. "You're not allergic to peanut butter, are you?"

I shake my head. "No." I cross the space between us and grab his face. When I kiss him, he makes a confused noise, but I ignore it. The heat between us expands. And a moment later, he's carrying me back upstairs.

"You really worked up an appetite," I comment as Nicolai swallows his third giant bite of food.

We're sitting on a giant quilt laid out on the grassy hill of a Saratoga park. The distant sounds of laughter and children shouting reach us from the playground on the other side of the park. A swing squeaks and a group of crows huddle near the varied spread Nicolai packed us for lunch. I gather my braided hair, pulling it forward so the mild wind can caress my neck.

"Actually, Ev," he says, setting down the empty paper his sandwich was wrapped in. "*You* really worked up my appetite."

I throw a balled-up napkin at him, a wry grin on my face. The light, happy feeling inside me is unfamiliar. Sitting here with him, free of worry for the future, feels too good to be true. I shake my head. "I don't get it, Nico."

"Well, you see, every time you kiss me, I want to—"

I cut him off with a giggle. "That's not what I mean." I fiddle with the ends of my braid. "I don't understand why you wanted to get to know me in the first place, after I first told you about my pregnancy. I get that Simone told you good things about me. But it doesn't seem like enough for someone like ..." I look him up and down. "For someone like you to want someone like me. It would make more sense for you to be completely turned off by my situation. A baby is a huge responsibility, and it's not even *your* responsibility."

He listens to me speak, lets me finish, and the remnants of humor fade from his expression. His eyes soften, and he reaches across the basket between us to capture my hand in his. "I get what you're saying. And I'm not going to lie. I *did* hesitate to get to know you when you first told me."

My heart struggles to continue beating. "You did?"

He nods. "But we had a connection. And I wasn't

willing to let it go because of a baby." He shrugs. "I've always liked kids. And shortly after you left my welcome home party, my mom told me something that kind of sealed the deal, as far as liking you went."

My brows furrow together. "What did she say?"

"She told me that she was in love with someone else before she married my dad. But he had a lot of baggage, so she let him go. She wanted to get married and start a family, but she wanted it to be with someone who had all the qualities she was looking for. Someone who looked good on paper. And then she found my dad."

I smile sadly, because I know what comes next. "But she didn't love him."

"No," he confirms. "She didn't. And after she told me that, she apologized to me for hurting me and Simone by leaving him. She made me promise something. That I would never throw away love like she did over something as superficial as a bad track record. And even though all we'd had at that point was really good chemistry, I knew I had to see it through." He rubs his thumb across my hand. "And I'm glad I listened."

"I'm glad you listened, too," I whisper. My throat is tight with emotion, but I rein it in. I pick up the basket and move it out of the way so I can sit close to him. He brushes a fleeting kiss to the side of my face and pulls me close. We sit, watching the children on the playground in the distance. For the first time since I got pregnant, the idea of my future doesn't lead to dread, but rather to the thing I've been searching for all along.

Hope.

TWENTY-FOUR

I don't dread work anymore. Not since Ashton found out about me stealing money. At first, I was nervous Willow would treat me differently, that she would scrutinize my every move in case I tried to steal again. But to my surprise, she's treated me fairly. And lately, she's scheduled me to work different shifts than Vaughn without me having to ask.

I can't even remember the last time Vaughn touched me. Last night he asked me when I would know if he's the baby's dad or not, and I told him the call should come at any time. And even though he swore nervously, the knowledge that I have Nicolai now comforts me. I don't have to worry about being stuck with someone like Vaughn, and honestly, I doubt he'd stick around anyway.

When I get home from night class, Mariah is on her knees under the dining table, picking up an assortment of crayons and colored pencils. "Amma! Get back here, please. I'm not cleaning up alone."

"Hey, Mom." I squat down to help her. "What's all this mess?"

"Amma was awarded the opportunity to illustrate a short comic for the school paper." She holds up a piece of paper with talking bears in a coastal landscape drawn out. "Look how good this is!"

Amma runs in, zipping up her pants. "Sorry. Bathroom emergency." She crawls under the table to gather the remaining pencils. "I'll get those."

"Good, because I'm sore tonight." Mariah gets to her feet, a hand on her lower back, and gives me a second, sharper look. "You look tired."

"I am." I'm always tired now, since getting pregnant. But it's still not the right time to tell her. Not until I get the results of the DNA test. She doesn't need to know the extent of my shitty situation.

There is something else I've been meaning to talk to her about, though. "Are you sure Dad's name was Leland?" I blurt.

She stills. "Of course. Why?"

I wonder if she's telling the truth. Maybe Leland is the one who lied to me. I hope so, because I can't bear the thought of her keeping me in the dark all this time. "I found your ex-boyfriend, Leland Jones, online. The one you claim is my dad. The one you said passed away before you could tell him about me." Her face is frozen in shock, but I continue. "I met with him. He denied everything, Mom. He says he's not my father."

She picks at a loose thread on the couch, unable to meet my eyes. And then she says something that pierces my heart like a knife. "I thought you'd never find out."

Without thinking, I back away from her.

"Listen to me." She holds her hands out, like I'm a crazed animal she's trying to calm. It's jarring to see her in this position: trying to mollify *me* for once.

But I don't want to listen. I shake my head. "I can't believe you lied to me!"

"I had to," she cries. "You don't understand!"

"Then enlighten me!" I shout. I've never spoken to her like this before. I've never, not once, yelled at her. But my brain is having trouble processing the fact that she hasn't been telling me the truth since I've been alive.

"Your father," she says, "your *real* father and his family can never find out you exist."

I blink. "What's that supposed to mean?"

"Please leave it alone, mija. Trust me on this. It's better if you never meet him."

"But Mom—"

"What's going on?" Amma asks. She's standing in the hallway, alarmed.

"Nothing," Mariah says. Her eyes plead with me to drop it.

I acquiesce. For now. But we'll be continuing this conversation when Amma isn't present. "Nothing," I echo.

Amma looks annoyed. "Whatever."

"I was about to order pizza," Mariah says brightly.

I pick up my phone. "I'll do it. Just get the coupons."

I flop onto the couch and stare at my phone, but my mind is elsewhere. *How could she keep all this to herself? Why wouldn't she just explain everything to me from the beginning?*

245

My phone chimes. It's Nicolai. *What are you eating for dinner?*

Me: *Pizza.*

Him: *Again?*

Me: *Yes. It's cheap.*

"Did you call them yet?" asks Amma from the table. She's working on her homework in the dining area now, probably in the hopes that we'll accidentally slip up and resume talking in front of her. "I'm starving."

I wave her off. "I'm about to."

"No, you're texting."

"Just be patient," I snap.

There's a knock on the front door. I hop up to answer it while simultaneously scrolling through my contacts to find the number for the pizza place we always order from.

Another text comes in from Nicolai. *I'm outside. I brought you guys real food.*

I open the door and there he is, with several bags of groceries in his hands.

I can't suppress the grin invading my face. I'm about to say something smart-assed when Mariah sees him from the kitchen. She runs and hugs him. "Nicolai! What are you doing here?"

He holds up the bags of groceries. "I brought dinner."

Her smile slips ever so slightly. I know what she's thinking. Nicolai knows how little money we have and is taking pity on us. And as nice as it will be to have food in our stomachs, my mother and I are the same; we don't like accepting things from people. Because at the end of the day, it never stops feeling like we owe them.

"You didn't have to do that," she insists.

"I wanted to." He takes the bags into the kitchen and puts them on the counter. Mariah turns on the stove and sorts through the food, putting perishables in the fridge and leaving the rest out.

I catch Nicolai's eye and gesture to my room. We walk down the hall and duck into my room. I shut the door behind us, and he immediately kisses me. His arms snake around my waist and his lips travel to my neck.

"Pizza would have been fine," I lie. But I'm not thinking about food. I'm hungry for something else.

"I wanted to see you. The groceries were an excuse."

"Consider me grateful."

I part his lips with my tongue. He moans into my mouth and I'm about to start taking his clothes off when he breaks away. "Your mom and sister are here."

"Fine." He's right. I need to get a grip and learn how to control myself. But looking at him, I want to tear his clothes off.

"Come over after dinner. Spend the night," he murmurs. "My mom officially moved out today."

"Your mom? Not your dad?"

"Yeah. She's been slowly taking stuff to her new place for a while, but today she got the last of it."

"I'll be there." I squeeze his hand.

"Thanks." The weight of his gratitude is clearly visible. *I know how it feels not to want to be alone,* I almost say, but the truth is, I haven't felt alone since I met him.

"Let's go back out there," he says.

In the kitchen, Mariah is cooking steaks—*steaks*—with baked potatoes while Amma puts salad greens in a large bowl.

"You're too much," I say to him.

He offers me a crooked smile, like it's no big deal.

"Everly," Amma says. "Your phone is ringing."

I track it down to where it's slipped between the couch cushions before it goes to voicemail. "Hello?"

"Hi, is this Everly?" a woman asks.

I walk to my bedroom and close the door. "This is her."

"This is Dr. Norman. I have your paternity test results."

"Oh!" My hand flies to my chest like someone from the eighteenth century. "Okay."

"To clarify, we have Subject A as Vaughn Lennard and Subject B as Johnathan Taylor."

"Okay," I say impatiently. "So, who is it?" A bead of sweat forms at my temple. *God, cut that toxic human from my life like the poisonous branch that threatens to infect the entire tree,* I pray silently.

"The test was positive for Subject B," she says pleasantly. "Jonathan Taylor."

John is the baby's dad? *John?*

I immediately picture John's eyes, how they'll shine when I tell him he's going to be a father. He'll smile, and it won't be his lips merely lifting, but a lighting-up of his entire face. He'll want to be involved every step of the way, be in the room when the baby is born, and pick out a name for his child.

His child.

And then the strangest thing happens. Something flutters in my abdomen. I gasp aloud and touch the spot.

"Is everything all right?" Dr. Norman asks.

Shit. I forgot she was still on the phone. "Yes," I say quickly. "Thank you." I end the call, put the phone down, and it happens again. It's like little bubbles are moving inside me, and it's the strangest sensation I've ever experienced. It makes all of this more real somehow.

"There's actually a baby in there," I say out loud. "Holy hell."

John's baby. Vaughn is off the hook.

I pick up the phone again and send him a quick text, because that's really all he deserves. *The baby isn't yours.*

His reply is instant. *Thank God.*

Thank God, indeed. I won't have to be tied to that monster for the rest of my life or be pressured to get rid of the baby.

Instead, I get John, who actually wants the baby, wants to get married and be a family. A happy, financially stable family.

Tears well up in my eyes because now that I know he's the baby's dad, it seems impossible to go back out there and continue with dinner, to smile at Nicolai and let him hold my hand. To throw away what might be the last chance to finally break my mother's mold in which I've been stuck since the day I was born.

I can't do this.

I can't be with Nicolai.

If I throw away this chance, this opportunity to give my child everything I've always wanted, I'll spend the rest of my life wondering what could have been.

It's no longer about me or what I want. If there's one thing I know about motherhood, it's that following my heart no longer matters. What I wanted became irrelevant the moment those two pink lines appeared.

A sob builds in my chest. I send John a text: *Can we talk tonight?*

He responds after a few minutes. *I'll pick you up in an hour.*

The tears fall down my cheeks, and my door opens, revealing Nicolai.

"Dinner's ready," he says. And then his eyes widen when he sees me crying. He's at my side in an instant, pulling me into a hug. "What's wrong? Is the baby okay?"

His concern makes my throat burn like fire with the effort to hold back a fresh round of tears. How do I tell him what I just found out? How is it going to make him feel to learn that all this time, my gut was telling me the baby was Vaughn's? And because of that, I never thought I'd be in this situation? That for once I didn't get stuck with what I deserve—the shittiest of all the options—and won the damn lottery instead?

My choice would have been easy if Vaughn was the dad. I could have told him to disappear and kept the baby. I'd raise it myself or with Nicolai and not feel a shred of guilt.

But John ... he wants all of it. And if I turn him away to be with Nicolai, I wonder if my child will ever forgive me.

"John is the baby's father," I croak.

Nicolai stiffens. "Oh."

"Sorry." I wipe my face. "I'm just emotional."

"Don't apologize. This is good, right?" His brows are drawn in confusion. "John is understanding and mature. He won't make this hard."

"We can talk more after dinner," I say evenly. "It will all work out."

He searches my face. "Okay."

We make our way to the table, and the smell of all the delicious food makes my mouth water. I sit across from Amma and Mariah. Mariah's gaze lingers on my eyes. I know she can tell I've been crying, but she clears her throat and pretends to refold the napkin on her lap.

Nicolai takes the seat next to me. Under the table, he holds my hand, moving his thumb lightly across the back of it.

Traitor, my heart tells me. *How can you hold his hand, knowing what you're about to do?*

But I ignore my heart and take a bite of the food. It's painfully delicious. I join in the conversation and laugh at the appropriate times, and when everyone has finished eating and the dishes have been washed, John texts that he's outside, waiting for me.

Just a few more minutes, I reply.

"Can we talk outside?" I ask Nicolai. "I'll walk you to your car."

"I thought you were coming with me."

"Not tonight." I open the front door, leading us out.

When we get to guest parking, John's expensive car is impossible to miss. Nicolai looks at it and then looks at me. My heart drops to my stomach when I see shocked sadness in his eyes.

"What is this?" he asks. "What's going on, Ev?"

I bite my lip. "Nicolai—"

"No. Don't do this. I know what you're thinking, and it's bullshit." He brings his head down to my level, so our gazes meet. "You don't need to be with him to be happy, and you know it. *I'll* make you happy. I promise. I'll love you and your baby as if it were my own." He grips my shoulders. "I already do."

My vision blurs. I can't take this. I can't stand the way he's looking at me, like his heart will fracture if I walk away. "I'm so sorry, Nicolai," I say weakly. "It's not the same. You have no idea what it's like not having a dad."

"Your baby will have a dad!" he yells. "Dammit, Everly. I'll be there, and so will John! Your baby will have two fucking fathers!"

I shake my head. I'm not sure who I'm trying to convince that he's wrong, him or myself. I'm shaking with the effort to hold it together.

John gets out of his car and joins us, looking troubled. "What's going on?"

"Nothing," I say. "Go back to your car, John. I'll be right there. I have to say bye to Nicolai and tell my mom I'm leaving."

John assesses the situation, looking between me and Nicolai, and nods. He gets in his car and turns off the engine.

"Try to understand how hard this is," I say to him.

His eyes harden. "I'm not going to beg you to be with me. If you want to leave me for *him*, that's your choice."

"It's the right thing to do."

Nicolai's jaw flexes. "If you say so." He averts his eyes, as if he can't bear to look at me anymore. And I know

252

what he's thinking. He's remembering, just like I am, what he told me: *The right thing is to follow your heart.*

Even though I want to scream at him—*It's you I love, you idiot! I'm doing this for my baby! Not because I want to be with John!*—I don't.

I can't.

When I finally break away from him, my heart throbs with each step I take. I wish I had my notebook, so I could write down what I'm thinking.

maybe hell isn't a place we go after we die,
but where we're already standing
the moment we
die
inside.

I don't look back as I walk to the apartment to see whether he's standing there, watching me go, or if he's already left.

I take a moment to collect myself before opening the front door.

Deep breaths, Everly. You can do this. Just tell them the news and leave with John. You can introduce everyone later, after you've had a chance to talk to him.

Mariah is right there when I open the door. When she sees me, her mouth falls open. "What happened? What's wrong?"

Behind her, on the couch, Amma is peering at me curiously, a small drawing notebook in her hand. I feel like I might vomit, so I blurt the words before I can back out.

"Mom," I say, "I'm pregnant."

TWENTY-FIVE

A week later, I'm ready to introduce John to my family. After I had finally confessed and dealt with their reactions, I was left too drained to introduce them. Especially since I still had to tell John he was going to be a father.

In addition to a lot of crying, there were a lot of questions and hardly any answers on my part. Every moment of procrastinating the introductions has since been filled with endless prodding from Mariah. *What are you going to do, Everly? When can we meet the baby's father, Everly? How are you going to take care of a baby, Everly? Have you considered adoption?* Endless, until I told her the father of my child happens to be very wealthy, very mature, and very committed. The three magic words, as far as she's concerned.

The only detail I happened to leave out was the fact that John is fifteen years older than me. I can't deny that our age difference doesn't thrill me, but I'm hoping it won't matter, considering all his positive attributes.

Like his car. The beautiful, black, Porsche 911 we're riding in on the way to introduce him to Mariah and Amma for the first time.

I grip his hand, my nerves kicking in. His support helps, but not enough to calm my stomach or wipe Simone from my mind. She's no longer speaking to me. After what I did to Nicolai, there's been nothing but silence. And I understand. She has every right to be mad at me. I broke a promise and hurt her brother.

I haven't heard from Nicolai since that night I chose John over him, either. It's been torture. Part of me thought he'd keep trying, even after I thoroughly ripped his heart out. His silence stings. I miss him. I miss his cheerful demeanor, his arms around me, his lips against mine. His genuine, uplifting laugh.

But I know that what I'm doing is the right thing. It just *has* to be.

"Don't be nervous," says John calmly. "I'm going to take care of you, and our baby is going to be so happy with us for parents."

I smile faintly, unable to meet his eyes. "I agree."

He's been talking constantly about how great things are going to be after the baby is born. At first it made me want to roll my eyes because it kind of felt like he was being unrealistic. Like he's happy to just have a substitute for what he's lost. But even so, it's starting to rub off on me, enough to make me actually imagine what life might be like *after* all this. A child. I'm going to have a child. The thought makes my head whirl.

"We should start planning our elopement as soon as possible," he states matter-of-factly. "We can get married wherever you like."

I blink. "Elopement?"

John smiles knowingly. "I'd love to give you a big, fancy wedding, Everly, but the amount of work involved would take too much time. You'd be showing."

"Oh. Okay, then. Elopement it is, I guess." I ponder what he said about being able to go anywhere. "I've always wanted to visit Mexico. See where my great-grandma grew up."

He nods. "Mexico it is."

We pull into my apartment complex, and I try not to wince at the contrast between his car and the shabby buildings around us.

John gets out and walks around to open the door for me. "Thanks." My stomach is heavy with dread, though there's nothing to worry about. John will be the perfect husband and father. He's a pediatrician and kind and will continue to be when this baby comes. My mom can't complain.

We climb the stairs, and I try to bury the memories of Nicolai coming over for dinner, picking me up the first time we went out to breakfast, the way I almost jumped him in my bed the last time he was here. I try, but the memories are still present, like a living, breathing person.

I'm walking up the stairs with a very different man now, my fiancé, who is readying himself to meet my family.

John knocks on the door, and Amma opens it, her eyes rounding slightly as she takes in John. I know what she's seeing: a tall white man in a crisp, ironed button-up shirt, slacks, and dress shoes on a casual day. A smile on his mature, clean-shaven face.

Amma holds out her hand. "Hi, I'm Amethyst, but you're allowed to call me Amma."

"Thank you. I'm John." He smiles warmly as he bends at the waist to shake her hand.

"He's the baby's father," I inform her. "Where's Mom?"

"In the kitchen. I'll go get her."

As we walk inside, he whispers to me, "I wish you wouldn't call me that. We're going to be husband and wife. You should call me your fiancé."

I shrug. "But you're also my baby's father."

He sighs.

I hear Amma in the kitchen also saying the words "baby's father," followed by Mariah turning off the stove. I usher John to the sofa and sit beside him while we wait for Mariah.

"Everly?" she says, rounding the corner into the living room. "Is he here?" Her voice is eager, excited.

We stand up and turn around to face her. "This is John, Mom," I say, the strength of my voice surprising me. "He's my baby's father *and* my fiancé." I grin at John, hoping he'll find amusement in my compromised title for him.

But John isn't looking at me.

He's staring straight ahead at my mom, his lips parted and his face bone-white.

I glance at Mariah and a chill races down my spine

when I see the same horror on her face. My pulse thunders in my ears. "What is it?"

She's breathing heavily, practically panting, and my unease blossoms into full-blown panic. Mariah releases a jagged moan that transforms into a scream so loud, I'm forced to cover my ears. Behind her, Amma's confusion and terror mirrors mine.

"Mom!" I yell. "What the fuck is going on?"

"Everly," John says, his voice gravelly and low, "this is your mother?"

"Y-yes." I'm truly frightened now because an unbelievable suspicion has planted itself in my head. "What are you talking about?" I ask, even though I already know the answer.

Mariah collapses to the floor, her face twisted into a grief-stricken grimace. "This is your father." She points at John.

Her words don't register. It's almost as if my mind is protecting me from the shock, from the horror, from the inevitable by dulling my senses and making her words sound foreign to my ears.

John is paler than ever. I realize belatedly that his eyes are wet. He doesn't look at me as he says, "No. *No.* This isn't happening. I can't believe you had her, Mariah! What the hell?" He yells the last part, and I jump. I've never even heard him raise his voice before.

When I finally allow myself to understand, the inevitable happens.

My vision blurs.

And goes completely black.

TWENTY-SIX
MARIAH

19 Years Ago

"John is too young for this," says Cecile. "And I want what's best for him. He's my son and that's all there is to it."

John's anxious eyes meet mine from across the living room. He's seated in an armchair next to his parents, who are on the sofa. "You can't decide that for us," he tells his mother.

His father, Howard, slams his fist on the coffee table. "The hell we can't! You have a future to fulfill, and no one is going to ruin that. Not even this slut."

My face burns in shame. I attempt to keep my chin up, though, to make him think his words didn't hurt me. But they did. They hurt so badly.

"How dare you," my dad bellows. "How dare you

speak about my daughter like that. She's not a slut. This is a teenage mistake. It happens."

Mama doesn't say a word. She's been crying silently into her sweater this entire time, completely overwhelmed and leaving me and Dad to do all the talking.

"Regardless, ending the pregnancy is probably the best solution for everyone," says Cecile, more softly this time, obviously trying to offset the outcry her previous statement caused. "It's settled."

I touch my stomach instinctively, the little bump that hasn't even had a chance to start moving yet has made me feel like there's someone in there, sharing my pain. I can't believe I've already grown so attached to it. John and I even started thinking of names last night, when we decided it was time to finally tell our parents. We chose John after him, if it's a boy. But for a girl, we came up empty. There was nothing good enough that we both liked.

I say around the thickness in my throat, "This isn't up to you. It's up to me and John."

Howard eyes me from behind his glasses. "Oh, really? And who's going to support either of you? I sure as hell won't. You can both end up in the streets as far as I'm concerned."

I straighten my back at his words. "My abuela did just fine when she came here. She worked her way up from the streets and took care of my mother when she got pregnant. She never even got married. She did it all on her own!"

John stares at me. His blue eyes are glassy, and I can't

look away. My heart breaks to see him like this when he's usually good at holding it together.

"Is that so?" Howard asks. There's an edge to his voice that makes my skin crawl. It's sinister enough to make me look away from John.

"Yes," I tell him.

"She never became a citizen of this country?" he inquires.

"No," Dad cuts in. "What does that matter?"

Howard smiles, but it's anything but happy. "It would be such a shame if she got deported after all this time."

"What did you say?" I whisper.

"My brother works for the Department of Homeland Security." John's dad looks pointedly at my stomach. "Have that baby," he challenges, "and find out what it's like to watch your grandma get taken away in cuffs and thrown back over the border."

Dad stiffens and Mom sobs even harder, slumping in despair. Tears well in my eyes.

Even Cecile looks uneasy. "Really, Howard?" she asks warily.

"Oh, I'm dead serious." He doesn't take his eyes off me. I'm not sure if what he's saying is true, if his brother has that kind of power, or if it would be as easy to accomplish as he's implying, but the picture he paints is painful enough to scare me.

John covers his face with his hands to hide that he's crying. "Dad," he begs. "Please don't do this."

"You're barely fifteen, Johnathan." His dad stands, signaling the meeting is over. "You'll thank me someday, son." To me, he says, "Do we understand each other?"

263

I want to spit in his face, but Dad pipes up before I can do anything I'll regret.

"She'll get rid of it," he says. "I'll schedule the appointment myself. You have nothing to worry about."

Cecile sags in relief, and they stand to walk us out.

Except John.

He remains in the armchair, his face a crumpled mess.

"Thank you, sweetheart," Cecile says kindly, rubbing my back. She has beautiful red hair, thick and shiny, that hangs just past her shoulders. I want to reach out and touch it, to see if it's as silky as it looks. Everything about her is soft, making me wonder how she can stand being married to such a hard man. "You'll have your chance again, when the time is right." I want so badly to believe her. She smiles at me like everything will be okay. But it's not a genuine smile; only an attempt at one to hide the subtle yet visible traces of pain.

We get in our car, and no one speaks at first. Mama's sobs have become sniffles, and Dad sighs deeply. "You are keeping that baby, Mariah."

I sit up. "But you just told them—"

"They'll never find out. They're never going to see any of us again, baby. We're moving."

Mama speaks for the first time, "Where?"

"Anywhere." His voice cracks. "We'll have each other. But Mariah," he says tensely. "You have to cut off all contact with John. He can never hear from you again unless you want to risk the chance of them finding out. I don't doubt for a second that John's father would retaliate in some way."

I nod quickly, my heart shattering. "We should go to California," I say. *California. The place John and I always dreamed of escaping to, where the beach is waiting like a long-distance lover. Where the sun transforms from Phoenix hell to comfortably warm.* The idea of California is a whisper, a remnant of the life we wanted together. It's what we could have had if things had played out differently.

Goodbye, John, I think. *I'm sorry I can't say it in person.*

But if I have to choose between him and Abuela, my own grandmother—between him and my baby—I'll say goodbye to him every time forever.

It's with those thoughts in my head, watching my old life pass by on the other side of the window, that I know exactly what I'll name this baby if it's a girl.

Everly.

I'm doing this for her. For Ever.

TWENTY-SEVEN

Dear Everly,
  He had ties to the Department of Homeland Security,
  she told you.
  To
  r e m o v e
  her would have happened in the
  blink of an eye,
  the simple batting of a lash.
  And you ask her
  where,
  you ask,
  is the security in that
  for those who call this land their home?

Time passes in spurts that I can't track. Spurts I don't
care to analyze. Pain is waiting for me if I wake up. I'd
rather stay in the darkness.

"Everly refuses to get out of bed," Mariah says.

John is my dad and the father of my child.

I drift into darkness again. I like it here. I want to stay.

Then I'm awake again.

"I'm sorry, I can't find a heartbeat."

I feel cold hands against my legs, prying them open, and something foreign enters me, searching my insides.

The baby.

"She fell on her stomach when she fainted." Mariah again, her voice a frantic, high pitch.

My baby with John is gone.

I know it when my body burdens me with the ability to hear the doctor's words. I know it when I wake from the darkness again, my stomach clenching in pain, the hot wetness of blood trickling down my legs after they've removed it from my body. The emptiness that follows could devour the world.

It's

g o n e

TWENTY-EIGHT

Dear Everly,

    I speak of grief as if we're old friends,
    but don't be fooled.
    We're not old friends. For I am grief, and she is me.

Dear Everly,

    what are you, they used to ask
    not who, but what
    as if to not be white
    was to not be human
    not what ethnicity, not what race
    but what
    what
    what are you
    & the worst part was
    you didn't even know
    yourself.

but you should have known
that you were a secret
all along
because
only Abuela knows Spanish
though she dares not utter a word
keep your roots hidden, she told you
don't give them a reason to label you
to think they've got you all figured out
don't let them know and they won't; they can't
they won't know where you come from
unless you tell them
so for God's sake,
speak like they do or
keep that mouth
c l o s e d.

I write in my notebook like a zombie. The entries and John's silence are my only markers of time since finding out he's my father.

He's been silent for a week, and I've been alive, though I'd much rather die. I'd rather never wake up than face what happened between me and him. Never face the fact that I sought him out and let him in, not knowing who he was.

I vomit. My body convulses with each upheaval, the bile landing on the floor beside my bed to which I've become permanently bound.

How could my mom not tell me? The thought is red and ugly in my mind, pointing fingers of accusation in her direction. *All of this could have been prevented if she'd told me the truth.*

But I know why she lied. I somehow remember the shouted words, wet and barely audible through the tears and tremors. "His parents threatened our family, mija. They wanted you aborted."

The stricken look on John's bone-white face, betraying no denial. His silence. It stretched out too long and still hasn't ended.

I don't know where he is.

He didn't show up to the hospital when the doctors scraped out my insides. *Stress,* they said. *This could have occurred from all the stress she's under. It wasn't necessarily the fall, which was minor. There hasn't been any severe damage to her abdomen.*

My phone rings. It's Nicolai.

I silence it.

He calls again and again, until it's clear I'm not going to answer, and the only thing left for him to do is leave a voicemail.

But when I see that there's a five-second recording of his voice, something happens.

I actually feel something.

I pick up my phone, press play, and lift it to my ear.

"It's me." I'm flooded with so many emotions when I hear his voice, I fear I might drown. "Your mom called Simone, and she told me what happened. I'm coming to see you."

I close my eyes. Nicolai is coming.

What exactly did he hear? Does he know that John is

my father? That the baby died, taking with it a sizable part of me too?

Mariah opens my bedroom door. "Mija, you have a letter." She comes inside, and I look at her, actually look at her for the first time since I brought John here to meet her. Her dark hair is in a braid, short strands in front escaping it, and her brown eyes are rimmed in red. Her lip is quivering, and I realize that she's afraid. Of what, though, I have no idea.

"Who is it from?" I hardly recognize my voice. It sounds flat, completely devoid of the emotion filling me like electricity through a live wire.

She sits at the foot of the bed and hands it to me. "From John."

I stare at the letter for a long moment before taking it. My hands shake. I start to open it, and she gets up. "I can't," she says, crying. "I can't be here when you read that." She covers her face with both hands before rushing out the door. I know I should feel sorry for her, but I don't. I really fucking don't.

I open the letter. The ultrasound photo I gave John falls out. A new knot forms in my throat. I grip it tightly and read the letter.

My dear Everly,

The day I met you, you walked up to me in a bar, and it wasn't a good day for either of us. I was mourning my wife, and you were celebrating your birthday alone. I took one look at you, at the expression on your face, and at that moment something happened. I had to know you. I don't know what it was about you—the eager expression in your eyes, the way you carried yourself, as if you knew exactly how beautiful you were but thought nothing of it. The carelessness of it all. I don't know.

Then you told me you stole money from your workplace, and I had to admire your honesty. There was this light about you that I hadn't felt inside myself for as long as I could remember. It was almost as if mine had been snuffed out, but being near you made me feel like maybe, just maybe it would be okay to borrow some of yours.

When you told me you were pregnant, some of that light entered me. And not your light, but my own, rekindling for the first time since I'd lost it.

When I was a teenager, I got my high school girlfriend pregnant, and my parents forced her to have an abortion. They claimed they were saving my future, making sure I still had a chance to live life. By their standards, I suppose they were right. I grew up without the responsibilities of being a young parent. I went to college and became a pediatrician. But, despite all these triumphs, I still never felt that light. It was snuffed out the moment Mariah disappeared from my life, taking with her the beauty we'd created together, whether it was an accident or not.

I married. I tried to have another baby, hoping that light would come back. Maybe if I had another chance to be a father, now that I'd done what my parents wanted, the light would return, and my life would finally have meaning. But after her three-year-long cancer battle, I not only lost my wife, but that hope, as well.

It seems horribly ironic, and horribly beautiful, that the light I lost disappeared when I thought my child was aborted. And that the first time I felt it again was when I laid eyes on you. My child.

You have to understand. I thought the light was the child you and I created together, but all along, it was you.

When I saw your mother again, I put it all together. I realized she never got rid of the baby. That she kept you hidden from me all these years. When I realized what I had done to you, what I had done to my only opportunity to know you, I realized I would no longer willingly walk this earth.

There are so many reasons why. There's my job, for one. As soon as word of this gets out—and it will—I'll be ruined. No one will trust me near their children again, knowing what happened between us.

There's your mother. I cannot face her. I can't look her in the eye, knowing what we did, knowing she has that same knowledge within her, too.

There's the baby, which has passed away. The doctors called me and told me. Though it feels like my heart has been ripped from my chest, I can't help but envy it.

And then there's you.

There's that light that is inherent in you, that I mistook as an opportunity to salvage the pathetic remnants of my life and turn them into something bright and burning, like the fire within you. I've ruined your chance of having a normal relationship with your father, of ever knowing me the way a daughter should know her dad.

You have to know, Everly. You have to know that I love you in the way a father should love his daughter. The love a parent has for their child simply cannot be surpassed. Everything was my fault, and I intend to salvage it. That is why I am removing myself from your life.

By the time you read this letter, I'll be dead, and it's okay.

I've wanted to move on for a long time, and what I did to you only reinforced my determination. Now you won't have to face me, because I can only imagine how much you're dreading it. All I can hope is that someday you'll find it in your heart to forgive me. That you'll possibly save this letter as a reminder that I love you. That you'll eventually be able to heal.

Goodbye, my daughter. I'm so glad we finally met.

In Peace at Last,
John Taylor

Mariah's screams begin before I've even finished reading, and my heart pounds so hard, I'm surprised it doesn't jump out of my chest. By the time I've read every word, I'm screaming too. How much can a heart take before the body ultimately kills it?

My mother's sobs grow louder as she approaches me. "He's gone, Everly." Pausing, she whimpers. "I just got a call from the police. He shot himself."

Even with my eyes closed, everything somehow gets blacker.

It's me again, I tell the darkness, and it welcomes me with open arms.

TWENTY-NINE

When I open my eyes, I realize I'm still alive. Somehow, this is the biggest blow of all.

Today is John's funeral, and I'm in my room, tucked under a blanket, alone. I don't remember how I ended up in such a peaceful position. Time has skipped like a stereo needle over a scratched record, leaving me with only bits and pieces of memory from the last few days. Or maybe it's been weeks. I can't remember. Nicolai showing up at my house to find me hysterical, gripping John's letter in a balled up, iron-tight fist...the soreness in my gut finally ebbing after my baby was removed...Mariah's silent presence in my room as she stared out the window like a stone carving, guarding me from who knows what. It's all a blur.

I am alone, and the thought is both pleasant and terrifying.

This is the first time I've been alone in over a month,

because even when I was alone, I wasn't. I had the baby inside me.

According to my mother, John left me everything: his house, his money, and his car. I don't want it, but I can't walk away from it without feeling like doing so is a slap in his face after everything he did for me. I won't have to worry about paying the electric bill for a long time. I'll never have to sell myself to keep a job. I should be happy. Ecstatic even, but all I feel is loss. To feel relief would be taking pleasure in his suicide.

Dear Everly,
  stay in pain, don't disappear
  for it's better to be hurting than missing
  better to be full of torment, of fear
  than empty, a shell reminiscing

My bedroom door crashes open. Nicolai marches in, eyes blazing. I can hear my mom's weak protests in the hallway. Her telling him I might want to be alone, that I'm still not doing well.

But he locks eyes with me, and I feel stronger.

It's good to see him again. So very good.

Hovering behind him, Mariah's eyes are wet, like she hasn't stopped crying all day. "Do you want him here? It's okay with me if it's okay with you."

"It's okay with me," I say steadily.

She nods, seeming somewhat satisfied with my answer. She walks away, and I try to speak, to say something to Nicolai, but I can't.

He walks over to my bed and scans my face, then he sits next to me and takes my hand in his. "I still can't believe it. I can't believe any of it." He pulls me against his chest when fresh tears spill down my cheeks. He holds me while I cry.

"Are you going today?" I whisper against his shirt. "To the funeral?"

"If you want me there, then I'm there."

"I do." I don't know how I'm supposed to wake up every morning and survive this sick joke my life has become without him.

I get ready in a daze, numbly applying a light coat of makeup to cover the redness around my eyes. I don't know why I bother. It's expected that people will cry. Still, I dab softly, makeup on my fingers, fingers against my skin, and shut my eyes against the flood of memories I keep trying to suppress. Of him. Of John. Thoughts and memories that aren't even tangible, but somehow more present than what's right in front of me.

Nicolai says behind me, "Where is your sister? Does she know what's going on?"

I shake my head. "She's with Chris's parents." I swallow hard. "My mom told her that everything was a mistake. Me thinking I was pregnant. John being the baby's dad. All of it. That sometimes doctors make mistakes." I turn to face him. "And she's right. This was all a mistake. One she could have prevented if she'd just been honest with me! But now she's lying to Amma, too, and everything's a mess." My hands tremble as I cover my face, and I sink to the floor.

"Hey." Nicolai kneels down next to me and rubs circles against my back. "Ev, it's going to be okay."

I grip Nicolai's shirt in my hands. "Then why," I gasp, "does it feel like nothing will ever be okay again?"

He presses a light kiss to the top of my head. "Because right now you're broken, but you're going to heal. When you do, you'll be stronger than ever."

The funeral is held at a church near John's house. The beautiful, two-story cathedral is complete with white marble carvings, a wood-pillared ceiling, stained glass windows, and a heavy, antique wood cross behind the priest. I haven't been to church in a while, but it feels really good to be back, like coming home after a long vacation.

My mother, Nicolai, and I find a mid-row seat, per my request. It's not like we would sit in front. As far as I know, no one close to John knew about us. It would have been unlike him to publicly announce his connection to me—or what he thought his connection to me was—before we'd had a chance to elope. Sitting in the back is almost as conspicuous as sitting in front, but sandwiched in the middle, we blend in.

I almost decided against showing up at all, but the idea of skipping it, without having a chance to pay my respects to John, hurt almost as much as his passing.

I fan myself with my hand to keep calm. The last thing I want to do is make a scene. I don't want anyone to notice me. I just want to get through the service and then get the hell out before anyone can ask me how I knew him.

Nicolai places a comforting hand on my knee. Gratefully, I place my hand over his. "Thank you for being here," I whisper. The ceremony hasn't begun yet, and people are still talking. There's something I've been wanting to ask Nicolai ever since that day in the cemetery, but I couldn't think of a good time to ask. Until now. "What happened to your birth mother?"

He looks surprised. "She suffered from a rare form of dementia shortly after I was born. She was having a difficult time caring for me, so she signed custody over to her sister and her husband, my parents now."

"How did you get through it when she passed away?" I search his face. "Did anything help the pain?"

He smiles sadly, searching my face. "She did the right thing. She loved me enough to give me to parents she knew would love and take care of me. I'm grateful to her every day for it. But honestly, Ev? Her death still makes me sad to this day. Every day hurts a little less than the day before, though. And one day, I realized my gratitude finally outweighed my sadness."

I nod. "I hope one day I can be more grateful than sad that I met John."

He squeezes my hand. "I hope that for you, too."

The ceremony begins, and it's pretty standard at first. A priest recites a eulogy from his book, and a few hymns are sung. Then some of the guests take turns saying a few words in remembrance of John. I listen to each person's words, wondering what kind of difference in his life these words would have made if they had been spoken while he was still alive.

I don't have my notebook with me, but it doesn't stop me from thinking the entry I would write if I did. *Dear Everly,* I think,

You're sitting in your seat, holding Nicolai's hand, listening to Mariah cry softly at your side, and it startles you, terrifies you, that one minute someone can be alive and then not alive the next. What does it even mean to be alive? Being alive isn't narrowed down to a singular action, like having a beating heart. Blood pumping through your veins. Because a machine can easily do those things for a person who is long gone, not there in their body anymore. As soon as the machine is unplugged ...

Being alive is something you can't wrap your head around.

There's something that cannot be seen by humans. Something buried beneath the layers of skin and tissue, bone marrow and blood. Something bright and burning.

Something loud and brimming with hope and impossible to ignore. Something that connects us humans, no matter how different the lives we lead or the origins that create the starts of our stories.

Something responsible for qualifying us as alive.

Everly, you can't help but call it a soul.

John's body may be dead, Everly. Your baby may be gone, too. But you know, you can feel that their souls are alive, out there somewhere in peace at last.

We stand to leave as soon as the service ends. I keep my chin tucked down in the unlikely event that I'm recognized. Mariah does the same. Nicolai leads the way face forward since he really doesn't have anything to worry about.

We're almost to the exit when Mariah trips on the edge of a pew, sending her crashing into a woman a few feet away. They collide and fall to the floor. Mariah recovers first and rushes to help the woman up.

"My goodness, I'm so sorry," she says.

"That's quite all right." The lady straightens her clothes and glances at my mother, then does a double take. "M-Mariah?"

She has steady blue eyes, and beneath the scarf tied around her head, a glimpse of shiny, thick red hair. I can't look away.

A man appears next to her and takes her elbow. "Is everything all right, Cecile?"

She ignores him. "Mariah?" she asks again, sounding hopeful this time. My mom nods, almost imperceptibly. I start to move forward, but Nicolai tugs on my hand. His eyes are a warning. "Wait. Be smart."

"H-how?" Mariah stutters. Glancing at the confused man next to Cecile, she says, "Howard."

He blinks. "Mariah?"

She turns to rush away, panic clear on her stricken face, when Cecile glances from her to me just as I say, "Mom?"

Cecile's lips part. She takes a few steps toward us, but Mariah makes for the exit.

This is exactly what we were trying to avoid. But looking at Cecile, I feel the invisible knowledge pass between the two of us. The recognition.

This woman is John's mother. My grandmother.

"Wait," I say and catch Mariah's sleeve. I understand why she's afraid. These are the people who were desperate to keep me from being born. They threatened to uproot my abuela, to tear our family apart so John could be free of his and Mariah's mistake.

I should be angry or afraid, just like my mom, but Cecile does the unexpected.

She pulls me into a hug.

Everyone speaks at once.

Howard: "Who is this?"

Cecile: "Is this who I think it is?"

Mariah, sounding small, but brave: "I couldn't do what you wanted. I just couldn't do it."

And then Howard again: "I'm so glad you didn't."

Silence.

The words hang in the air between us, healing wounds I didn't know existed, injuries we'd grown accustomed to living with.

I pull away from the iron hug Cecile holds me with. "Maybe we could all go to lunch together? Talk about things?"

She looks at me again, this time with an added layer of emotion. "Let me look at you," she whispers. "Oh my word, you're stunning. Absolutely beautiful."

I smile, but it's layered with sadness. Because I know what she's really saying: *I see my son in you.*

I finally gaze at Howard, who's having a hard time looking at me. "Hello."

This towering old man with sagging skin and age spots looks exactly like John. And he, too, is crying.

Cecile links an arm through mine. "Lunch sounds wonderful."

THIRTY

5 Years Later

The memory of John and the baby we lost still hurts. I don't think it will ever stop, if I'm being honest. But instead of crippling, incapacitating pain, the ache in my heart has settled into a manageable throb.

I'm okay.

Better than okay, at the moment. Because I never thought in a million years I'd be sitting here with Simone, in the apartment Nicolai and I rent together, addressing invitations for my college graduation. I dreamed about this moment many times, but I never truly believed I could pull this shit off.

"Your ring is extra sparkly today," Simone comments. She licks an envelope and seals it, then places it in the pile of invitations that are ready to be mailed. She and Nicolai teased me for wanting to invite people the old-school way, with *paper*. And I admit, it would have taken much less time to send electronic invites. But licking the envelopes closed and addressing each one by hand feels satisfying. Each letter I address is like another *I did it, I did it* in my head.

Plus, I knew my grandparents would appreciate it.

Ever since lunch that day after John's funeral, Mariah and I have maintained a healthy relationship with Howard and Cecile Taylor. Neither of us have explained the extent of what happened between me and John. I'm not sure we ever will, and I'm okay with that.

I never thought I would have the chance to get to know my father's family, or that there would be another good or happy moment in my life again after his passing.

I was wrong.

I glance at the ring on my left hand, and a flood of memories crowd my mind. Specifically, the moments leading up to the day Nicolai asked me to marry him. How, after the darkest period of my life, I never got out of bed or smiled, and Amma noticed.

"What happened to her?" she had asked. "What's wrong with Everly?"

"She's just hormonal," my mom said.

Lying yet again, though this lie I understood.

Eventually I stopped sleeping all day. I made an effort to smile when people were looking. I continued college. I got to know my new grandparents and allowed them to get to know me. They made amends with Mariah and her parents, and the emptiness inside me filled.

A year passed, and when my mother was finally well

enough to wean off antidepressants, she apologized for lying to me all those years about who my dad was, for making me believe he died, so I wouldn't go searching for him. "This all could have been prevented," she said. "If only I had told you these things, mija."

I had already felt at peace with Mariah and my own actions. I didn't feel that confronting Mariah fully would benefit me. But somehow, her apology helped.

After that my heart started to heal.

The distractions that school provided helped. At first, I was set on engineering, but when Nicolai reminded me I'd only wanted to do that for the money, he'd looked pointedly at my notebook and said, "You should major in what you feel passionate about," and I realized he was right. I buried myself in writing and I loved every second of it.

Simone eventually reached out to me, apologizing for turning her back on me when I needed her most. "You have nothing to apologize for," I said. "I probably would have done the same if it were Amma."

"I finally confronted my parents," she said when we hung out again. "I asked them if I could have the business."

"And they said yes?"

"They did." Simone gritted her teeth. "But they wanted to give Nicolai first dibs. Like he knows anything about business. I'm practically a freaking CEO, and they want to offer it to him."

I laugh. "Yeah, that's bullshit."

"What else is new? But they finally came around and realized he has no interest."

If it weren't for Simone's parents constantly bickering over who would keep the house, because both refused to sell, Nicolai probably wouldn't have been as desperate to move out.

I, however, wanted to leave town. Hell, I wanted to see a state other than California. When he suggested we move to New York, I jumped at the opportunity.

But first, I did something I should have done the moment it happened. I went to the police and reported everything Vaughn did to me. And the moment the confession left my lips, I wondered why I hadn't done it sooner. At least now, he'd be less likely to do it again to someone else.

I rented out John's house, put his car in storage, and transferred my classes to NYU. Nicolai went through the process of transferring his teaching credentials so he could teach at Lower Manhattan Middle School. Mariah was upset when I told her I was leaving, and I felt bad for her. But my heart broke when I had to say bye to Amma. "You're coming to see me once a month," I told her at the airport, the sight of her tear-stained cheeks forming a knot in my throat. "I'm flying you out, since I have lots of money now."

"You should probably donate it to charity," Amma said. "You're much too careless to be rich."

After moving into a tiny Brooklyn loft and adjusting to city life, it happened. Things got even better.

I was walking through Central Park with Nicolai one afternoon, marveling at the sheer size of it. After less than a mile, my feet were burning. "I should have worn different shoes," I complained, glancing at my flats with contempt. Nicolai bent down to tie his shoes. "You should have, too."

He laughed. "Want me to carry you? Because I can totally carry you."

An image of me slung over Nicolai's shoulder flashed through my mind. "As tempting as that is, I'm actually good."

We walked until we reached Bow Bridge, where Nicolai kneeled to tie his shoelaces for the third time.

"Double knot them," I suggested.

But this time, instead of standing back up, he remained on one knee, and a tiny box appeared in his hands.

I stared at him. He stared right back.

"Yes," I blurted. My heart raced, so fast, I thought I was going to pass out. He looked perfect in that moment, like a statue carved out of the bridge, meant to stay there for eternity. "I'll marry you, Nicolai." My eyes shined. "You don't even have to ask."

He removed the ring from the box. "I want to ask. Don't take this from me, Ev."

I pressed my smile between my lips, but it still broke through, dammit. "Okay. Go ahead."

"Everly," Nicolai began. "Everly Jean Martin. The day I met you, you abandoned me at an empty Beanbags table, two drinks in hand. I decided you were too weird for me, and it was a good thing you left before I could get attached. Then I found out you were Simone's friend, and you became off-limits. But you got under my skin, and I'm glad. You're the best thing that's ever happened to me, and I love you. I love you so much."

My eyes filled with tears. I wanted to scoop him up off the ground and kiss him, but I let him finish.

"Will you marry me?" he asked. "Will you be my wife?"

My breath caught in my throat. "Yes, Nicolai. I will."

He stared at me for the longest moment, the look in his eyes like that of someone witnessing the impossible. And then he stood, cradled my face gently in his hands, and kissed me.

Whatever shattered remnants my heart had become, I placed into his hands that day. My last two pennies.

When I gaze at my ring now, I can't help but think about all the things that led up to this, the day I'm sending out graduation invites.

"You're staring at it again," Simone says. "Haven't you done that, like, a thousand times by now?"

"Shut up," I say lovingly. "One day, when you and Kiley are engaged, you'll do the exact same thing."

She's silent for so long, I turn around and glance at her. "Oh, God, you didn't break up, did you? I'm so sorry. I'm such a dumb bitch."

She cracks a smile. "Actually," she says, "I'm proposing when I get back to Cali. I was going to ask you later to help me pick out a ring."

My mouth falls open. Then I stand and throw my arms around her in a giant hug.

It's at that precise moment that Nicolai walks in, and as soon as our gazes lock, I feel the flutters that I experienced the first time he smiled at me all over again.

He sees me hugging his sister and crosses his arms. "What did I miss?"

Simone shakes her head ever so slightly, as if to say, *Not yet.*

"Nothing much. How was work?"

"Good." He wraps me in his arms, pulling me flush against him. "But I'm glad to be home."

Simone readies to make her exit. "And that's my cue. See you guys later."

"You're leaving already?" I ask.

"Don't worry." She grins at me. "I'll see you tonight. For that *thing*, remember?" And then she's gone.

Nicolai eyes me suspiciously. "Thing? What thing?"

"*Nothing*," I insist. "She'll tell you when she's ready. Sometimes girls tell their best friend stuff first. Get used to it."

My answer must be sufficient because he nuzzles my hair. "Speaking of getting used to things," he murmurs, "you'd think I wouldn't get this riled up every time I see you."

"That's only fair. It's the same for me." I pull him into our room and playfully shove him onto the bed.

He kisses my neck and collarbone, and I stroke his golden hair, the silky strands caressing my fingers.

We remove our clothes, and I can feel every inch of his skin against mine. He pulls my legs up, around his waist. "Show me what you got," I tease.

He doesn't disappoint.

Afterward, he asks softly, "You took your pill, right?"

I nod, and he tightens his arms around me. He knows I may never be ready to get pregnant again, but the emotional scar from losing the baby is beginning to fade.

When that time comes—*if* it comes—I'm absolutely sure I want it to be with Nicolai.

Before I fall asleep, I untangle myself from the arms wrapped tightly around me and take out my journal.

For years I thought I was alone and that no one else was here to listen, that no one else gave a damn.

But I was wrong. It was never that no one gave a damn, but rather that I never let them.

I flip open my notebook and read the most recent entry. It's short, but it fills me with hope.

Dear Everly,

Today you are too heavy for yourself to carry. But you have learned that God will gladly take the weight from you, if only you will hand it over.

I write one last letter to myself, because for the first time, I know in my heart I'm being heard by others, too.

Dear Everly,

I am still grief; she is still me.

But that's not all I am.

I'm silence, spoken, happy, sad,

still falling, though I stand.

I'm full of awe and wonder, and some indifference.

Full of laughter, full of crying, and a bit of confidence.

Where I was once left empty, nothing more than grief,
I'm slowly filling up again.
I'm rousing from my sleep.
Dear Everly, stop trying so hard to be complete.
It's better to be free and walking on your feet.
With freedom there's acceptance that comes from deep within
and even better, love, which conquers every sin.
Those pennies were worth giving, those pieces of my heart.
What I got back was hope and a new chance to restart.
I don't want to go back to that person from before.
I must keep moving forward. I must become much more.
I promise I'll keep trying
in every storm I weather,
I promise I'll keep trying
forever and for Ever.

RESOURCES

Dear Reader,

If you or someone you know struggles with thoughts of self-harm or suicide, or could use help leaving a dangerous situation, here are a few 24/7, confidential, and free resources.

Thank you for making this world a brighter place. You matter and are so loved.

National Suicide Prevention Lifeline: 1-800-273-8255 or visit https://suicidepreventionlifeline.org.

National Sexual Assault Hotline: 1-800-656-HOPE (4673) or visit https://www.rainn.org.

National Domestic Violence Hotline: 1-800-799-SAFE (7233) or visit www.thehotline.org.

ACKNOWLEDGMENTS

First and foremost, I'd like to thank God. Thank you, God. I love you.

Next, my husband. Michael, thank you for always supporting every single crazy idea that comes into my head, invited or not. If it weren't for you, this book wouldn't even exist.

My kids, Oliver and Phoebe—thanks for sharing your mommy with so many fictional characters. I love you both so much.

To my mom—thank you for always being there when I need you. Your ears are probably crammed full of bookish nonsense by now, but you still listen to every word with such enthusiasm.

My cousin, Ashley, thank you for always being my reading and writing soul mate. I could't write a single word without you. You're more essential to me than the computer I'm typing this on.

My cousin, Haley, thank you for lending me your genius mind and letting me pick it apart without hesitation. I could talk to you all day and feel like no time at all has passed.

To my amazing beta readers, author friends, and critique partners—thank you for your endless support.

Wendy Higgins, Cre'shea Hilton, Suzy MacDonald, Laura Shiff, Katie Shoun Cingel, Chelle, Fen, Lillian Schneider, Marissa Taylor, Taylor Rowan, Tiffany & Troy Donovan, and Oriana Castillo—thank you so much for helping this story grow and flourish. You're all amazing and I'm so grateful for you.

Thank you to Murphy Rae and Ashley Ranae for creating such a beautiful cover. My eyeballs are so happy, yet again.

My whole family, thank you for always being so supportive. Grams, thank you for believing in me and I know you'd be proud if you were still here. Thanks to the love, encouragement, and memories you left behind, it feels like you never left.

And finally, thank *you*, my amazing reader. You're the one who makes every word worth it. I love you.

ABOUT THE AUTHOR

 Whitney Amazeen's love for reading started in third grade and has been going strong ever since. She studied cosmetology before pursuing writing, where she used to hide in the laundry room to read and write instead of working on clients.

As a result, Whitney has evolved into a full-fledged daydreamer with more stories in her head than she can count. When she's not immersed in reading or writing a novel, Whitney spends the majority of her time playing with her kids and watching Disney movies.

Whitney lives in California with her husband and two children and can often be found drinking tea, hoping for foggy weather, and obsessing over fictional characters.

Learn more at WhitneyAmazeen.com
& Sign up for Whitney Amazeen's newsletter to be notified of new releases!

instagram.com/WhitneyAmazeen

tiktok.com/@whitneyamazeen

goodreads.com/WhitneyAmazeen

amazon.com/author/whitneyamazeen

bookbub.com/profile/whitney-amazeen

Loved *Something Bright and Burning*? Don't miss *One Carefree Day*,
in which eighteen-year-old Willow Bates must attempt to
control the rituals ruling her life. Either she manages her OCD,
or she loses her home. What she doesn't expect—finding love
in the process.